Warlocks

ELEMENTAL LOVE

L.M. SOMERTON

Elemetal Love
ISBN # 978-1-78651-939-9
©Copyright L.M. Somerton 2016
Cover Art by Posh Gosh ©Copyright March 2016
Interior text design by Claire Siemaszkiewicz
Pride Publishing

Published in 2016 by Pride Publishing, Newland House, The Point, Weaver Road, Lincoln, LN6 3QN, United Kingdom.

Pride Publishing is an imprint of Totally Entwined Group Limited.

ELEMENTAL LOVE

Dedication

For anyone who needs a little magic in their life.

Prologue

Twenty-one years ago…

"Closed doors, I hate closed doors. Why don't I have the power to see through them? That, at least, would be a useful ability." Three-hundred-year-old floorboards creaked as Gregory Thanet paced the galleried landing of Wenlock House. He walked up and down past three doors, each fashioned from heavy oak and furnished with black iron hinges and handles. Two stood ajar, revealing hints of unoccupied bedrooms, but the third was firmly closed, a solid barrier to unwanted intrusion and the cause of Gregory's current frustration.

"For goodness' sake, Gregory, you're wearing out the carpet. Be still." Gregory's companion leaned against the gallery rail and gave him an exasperated look.

Gregory paused his march briefly, shot a glare at the woman but then resumed his pacing with a grunt. "Leave me be, woman, I'll be still when we know that everything is as it should be."

"Nature moves at her own pace, you know that. There's no changing it—nor should we. What will be will be."

"Stop trying to sound like some wise and ancient soothsayer, Agatha. You're not helping and it doesn't suit you. The kid is a week late already—you'd think he would be keen to greet the world by now. When he's grown I'll remember that he kept me up half the night. I'm sure I'll get plenty of opportunities for revenge when he's older." Gregory stopped and folded his arms across his chest.

"I might not be able to see the future, Gregory Thanet, but even a complete idiot could have predicted that my grandson would arrive today."

Gregory examined his companion. Agatha looked tired. Her skin was quite smooth, marred only by a few laughter lines around her hazel eyes, eyes that still sparkled with warmth and intelligence. Her silver hair was swept smoothly back and fastened with a comb, intricately fashioned from beaten copper. She remained an attractive woman, who must have possessed great beauty in her youth, but she looked paler than usual and she rested her weight against the banister rather than standing in her usual ramrod-straight stance.

Gregory experienced a rare pang of guilt that he might be adding to his friend's worries. "All Hallows' Eve. There's a lot of power in the air right now."

Agatha cocked her head to one side and closed her eyes as if listening to sounds that only she could hear. "My grandson will be with us soon and there is little that you or I can do to change the course of his destiny." For a moment, a worried frown creased her forehead. "It is not certain that he will inherit the gift."

Gregory sighed. "In this, you deceive yourself, Agatha. The calling has skipped a generation. History dictates that the next born will be unusually powerful and that power will be magnified even further in a male child."

"There has been no warlock in my family line for over five hundred years, only witches. Why are you so convinced that it will change now? We know of only three others living, Gregory. You, Symeon Malus and Constantine De Vries. It would be a chance in a billion."

Gregory scratched the tip of his long nose. "I should have bought a lottery ticket then. All the portents point to it, the date alone... It is time. Time the triangle became a square."

"I'm not sure Symeon Malus will ever be part of that square," Agatha said. "I don't see him as the cornerstone of anything with value or integrity."

"True, and if the child is born with the power, you and I will need to ensure that Symeon's gaze remains elsewhere." Gregory shivered. "I swear to the goddess, this country is the dampest place on earth. It's all right for you, Agatha, you live in the second dampest place on the planet. You're used to groping through fog. I want to get back to Florida. I need to — before I develop trench foot."

"Pah. What you really want is to get back to Coryn. You're a ship without an anchor when the two of you are apart. He could have come to see the child too, you know." Agatha grabbed a stray hair and pushed it back into a restraining grip.

"Coryn hates airplanes, you know that. I would never ask him to fly across the pond unless it was a life or death situation."

"If it were, you wouldn't *have* to ask him."

"He reckons that if men were designed to fly through the air, then human cannonball would be a much more popular career choice."

Agatha snorted. "I think his phobia is a myth. He just uses it as an excuse to get a few days' break from your—" She whistled and twiddled her fingers in the air.

Gregory rolled his eyes. "Twiddling your fingers that way will get you turned into an aardvark. It takes practice to bend your digits into shapes imbued with power. After thirty-two years together, Coryn is more than capable of dealing with my—" He whistled. "As you so delicately put it."

Agatha snorted. "Men with magic! Whoever the hell thought that would be a good idea was seriously damaged." She shook her head slowly.

Gregory grinned and waggled a silver eyebrow.

The mewling cry of a newborn sounded from behind the closed bedroom door, and Agatha allowed her lips to curve into a smile.

"Well, it seems the waiting is over. I have a grandchild—and, from the sound of that bellowing, he's a fine, healthy boy."

"About damned time." Gregory grouched. He still smiled right along with Agatha.

Agatha crossed the landing and knocked softly on the door, which soon swung open to admit her. Gregory followed her inside, pushing down his excitement.

The bedroom was bathed in the cool light of a new dawn. The soft green of the walls seemed to shimmer and the wooden floor was burnished with gold. Gregory looked around in wonder, then dragged his gaze back to the bed.

"Lyssa, James—congratulations, my dears!" Agatha clapped her hands together in delight as she walked over to the bed.

Gregory hung back a little, giving her the privilege of first viewing.

Agatha's daughter, Lyssa, sat up in bed propped against a mound of pillows. She was pale, her eyes shadowed in the purple of exhaustion, but still she glowed with radiant happiness. A small bundle wrapped in a pale blue blanket rested in her arms. Her husband, James, sat nervously on the edge of the mattress, looking utterly shell-shocked but delighted as the midwife fussed around them.

Lyssa held the baby out to her mother with a smile. "His name is Evrain. Evrain James Brookes. Hold him, Mum, isn't he beautiful?"

Gregory held his breath as Agatha reached for the small bundle and cradled the child in her arms. She pushed the blanket back from the baby's head, and a mop of thick black hair was revealed, sticking out in all directions.

"He is absolutely gorgeous, darling. Didn't you both do well!" Agatha stroked the child's hair.

Gregory moved in closer. Tiny fists punched at the air, so Gregory offered the boy his own hand. Immediately, the baby grabbed hold, wrapping his fingers around Gregory's offering with surprising strength. Gregory grinned at Agatha in delight, then looked back to the baby. His eyes were the dark blue of every newborn but, as Gregory focused his senses on the child, he could see that they would become dark green. Just a shade deeper than his own.

Cooing softly, Agatha muttered a lilting incantation and rocked the baby gently. To Lyssa and James, the song probably sounded like a lullaby, but Gregory knew a spell when he heard one. Tiny eyelids closed and the baby slept. Gregory's finger was released. After a few more minutes of cuddling, Agatha reluctantly returned the baby to his parents.

"He's absolutely perfect, Lyssa, love. I'll leave you to rest now, I'm sure you must be exhausted. Look after her, James."

"Of course," James replied. "She'll be a pampered lady of leisure from now on."

Lyssa nearly choked laughing. "Oh, James, I think you are in for a big shock. I can't wait to see you change your first nappy or clean up some projectile vomiting."

"Hey, don't spoil my idealized view of the world, I have my rose-tinted specs firmly in place."

"As all new fathers should," Gregory said, shaking James' hand.

Agatha tutted. "It's been a long night. I, for one, am looking forward to my bed."

"Thanks, Mum. I'm so glad that you and Gregory are here. It's made all the difference having you both around."

The midwife hovered, her face a studied mask of professional patience, but Gregory knew he was about to be ejected. He took a last peek at the sleeping child then led the way from the room, ushering Agatha through the door before closing it behind him. He didn't have a chance to utter a word. Agatha took his arm and pulled him downstairs to the kitchen. As she put the kettle on, Gregory sent her a questioning glance.

"Well? I caught the spell you did. Does that mean what I think it does?" Gregory asked.

She nodded. "It has come to pass. My grandson has the potential to become one of the most powerful warlocks ever known. His aura is shockingly bright." She busied herself making herbal tea. Gregory recognized her fear and her need for distraction. He let her potter without interfering.

"Less than an hour old and it is already evident to me that he will possess terrifying power," Agatha said. She held up a bony hand to still Gregory's questions. "I have placed a shielding spell on him—no evidence of his abilities will manifest until he passes the age of twenty-one. We can only pray that by then he will have the strength to accept what he is and to face his future."

Gregory sighed. "When he comes of age, we must do what we can to guide him. If he breaks under the strain and turns to the wild magic, we will have no choice but to destroy him."

Agatha nodded and handed him a mug of tea. "Agreed. I accept this duty—he is my blood. I will do all I can to lead him down the right path and protect him from those who will wish him harm. But I need your help too, Gregory."

Gregory nodded.

"He will need guidance from another warlock. I don't have the skills to teach him everything he'll need to know."

His hands suddenly cold, Gregory gripped his mug tightly. "I may not be a blood relative, but you and yours are still my family, Agatha. You have my word... I will do everything in my power to keep him safe. To teach and guide him."

They fell quiet and steam from their pungent drinks misted the air.

Chapter One

Present day

"You didn't have to babysit me, Gregory. I'm quite capable of traveling alone, even if it is transatlantic." Evrain glanced at the man seated next to him in the luxurious first-class cabin. "Not that I don't appreciate the ticket. I could get used to this. I usually get stuck in the back row with the delights of eau de chemical toilet."

His godfather's seat was slightly reclined. Gregory's eyes were closed and a couple of faint lines furrowed the bridge of his nose. He opened one eye, revealing a slither of pale green.

"Is it over?" Gregory asked.

"Is what over?" Evrain asked in confusion. They had only been in the air ten minutes.

"Takeoff. I hate it. My stomach always stays on the tarmac while its contents journey in the wrong direction up my esophagus."

"Ugh, gross!" Evrain groped in the pocket next to his seat and extracted a pristine paper bag. "Do you need this?"

Gregory opened his other eye. "No. But I could use a Bloody Mary. Where's the trolley-dolly?" He jabbed at the call button.

"I'm sure he'll be around in a moment. Give the poor guy a chance. He's probably still strapped in his seat. I thought it was Coryn who didn't like flying?"

"He loathes it, poor dear. I am entirely indifferent. It's just the upping and downing parts that don't agree with me. I have a delicate constitution."

Evrain snorted. "Bullshit, Gregory. I've seen you down half a bottle of Jack alongside a pint of Rocky Road ice cream and that's a combination that's probably banned under international law. If it isn't, it should be. You have a cast-iron stomach."

"We have a wide range of beverages, sir, but that's not a combination I can offer, I'm afraid. Nor would I advise it."

Evrain, who was sitting in the aisle seat, turned to the air steward standing next to him. The man had a huge grin on his face and a trolley stacked high with miniature bottles of every type of booze known to man.

"Something we can be thankful for," Evrain said. "Could we have a couple of virgin Bloody Marys please?"

"Make that one virgin and one fully confirmed slut," Gregory grouched. "Which category do you fall into, sweetheart?" he asked the steward whose name badge declared him to be called Samuel. A pair of pretty hazel eyes sparkled.

"I can see I'm going to have trouble with you, sir."

He was cute. Not Evrain's type, but the sandy hair that flopped into his eyes was endearing.

"Behave, Gregory, or I'll tell Coryn." Evrain swiveled back toward the aisle. "He's married, Samuel, and old enough to know better."

The steward mixed their drinks and handed them over. "Call me Sam. I fully intend to grow old disgracefully myself. Perhaps you could give me a few tips?" The last remark he aimed at Gregory.

Gregory opened his mouth but Evrain jumped in. "Please don't get him started, Sam. You'll still be here in eight hours' time and I'm sure the other passengers have need of your services."

Gregory pouted. "Stop spoiling my fun, Evrain."

"You're sixty-five, not six, Gregory. You're supposed to be keeping an eye on me, not the other way around."

Samuel gave them a couple of menus. "Here are the choices for lunch. Please have a think about what you'd like and I'll be back in twenty minutes or so to take your orders." He pushed his trolley to the next row and began to chat to the passengers seated behind Gregory and Evrain.

Evrain wasn't particularly hungry. He put the menu aside. "Why don't you tell me something about my new home? I've done a bit of research on the net, but I'd like to hear about it some more."

Gregory downed his drink in a single gulp. "Christ, I needed that." He smacked his lips together. "You've stayed with Agatha dozens of times, you know the area pretty well by now I'd have thought."

"It's true I spent most of my school holidays with her, but she rarely took me out of Hood River. I'm going to be living in Portland, which I don't know very well at all. I think I've been there twice. I'm starting a job with a company I interviewed for over Skype—and don't pretend you didn't have some influence over that, Gregory, because I know you did. What firm takes on a new graduate with no experience on the basis of a forty-five minute conversation?"

"One with a chief designer that knows talent when he sees it." Gregory fiddled with his empty glass.

Skeptical didn't even begin to describe how Evrain felt about that statement. "You can't lie for crap, Gregory."

Gregory sighed. "That's Coryn's fault. He always knows when I've been bullshitting him and he has this look."

"Look?" Evrain cocked a quizzical eyebrow.

"You know. That whole narrowed eyes 'tell me the truth or you're sleeping on the couch' look."

"He makes you sleep on the couch? Even after how many years together?" Evrain chuckled. He loved the idea that Gregory had visited the doghouse, a place Evrain was all too familiar with.

"Almost forty years. Forty amazing, astonishing, unbelievable years. Something I hope you'll have with someone one day, Evrain."

Evrain was tempted to tease his godfather but the wistful, dreamy look in those normally cool eyes stopped him.

"I can't imagine what it must be like to spend so many years with one person. Coryn deserves some kind of award for putting up with you for that long."

"Time is a strange thing. When you're young and curious, it drags its heels. When you're old and crotchety like me, it speeds past in the blink of an eye. Make every moment an adventure, Evrain. Don't let the weight of responsibility bow those young shoulders before their time."

"Wow, getting a bit deep there, Gregory. Why don't we get back to what you were lying through your teeth about?"

"Ah. Well. I suppose I should confess that I do have a small stake in ThInk."

"A small stake. What exactly does that mean?" Evrain forced himself to keep his voice low. "You have a few shares in the place, or you were best man at the chief executive's wedding?"

"I might own the company," Gregory mumbled.

"You own it. The whole company. Well, fuck." Evrain downed the rest of his drink in one and regretted the lack of alcohol. "Unbelievable. Grandma's been trying to persuade me to move to the States for the last three years. Is this all a collusion between the two of you to get me out of the UK?"

"Get off your high horse, boy. I showed Chip Franklin some of your work. It was his decision to offer you an interview. I had nothing to do with it."

"You're not messing with me? Because I can get off this plane in Seattle, buy a new ticket and head straight back across the pond, you know."

"Evrain, I don't want to swell that already cocky head of yours, but you have talent. You graduated a year early, for Christ's sake. Your work is original, fresh... Perfect for a company like ThInk. Chip isn't stupid. You'll bring in big commissions and make him look good to the board. If he didn't think you were worth the investment, he would have had no hesitation in kicking you into touch."

Evrain slumped in his seat and tried not to smile. Pride had his lips twitching.

"I *am* good, aren't I?"

Gregory rolled his eyes. "And arrogant with it. It's time you learned to deal with the real world. It'll do you good."

"Hey, it's hardly my fault that I've never had the chance." Evrain picked at a loose thread in the seam of his black jeans. "You and Grandma saw to it that all my holidays were fully occupied. I could have stayed at home and flipped burgers to earn some pocket money."

"The last time I ate one of your burgers at a family barbecue, I almost broke a tooth. It was like chewing on a lump of coal."

"Flames don't like me, you know that," Evrain protested. "It just got away from me, and, before you ask, no I didn't throw extra fuel on it."

"Oh, believe me, I know you didn't."

Evrain gave his enigmatic godfather a sharp look. "Why is it that I always get the feeling there are double meanings in half the things you say? Grandma is just as bad. I'm convinced there's some deep, dark family secret that you're both keeping from me."

Gregory drummed his fingers on the armrest of his seat. "What's on that lunch menu? I'm starving."

Evrain growled. He knew it was pointless to carry on interrogating Gregory. Once his godfather decided to clam up, there was no prizing open his lips. He retrieved his menu.

"Roasted cod, minted lamb shank or spinach and mushroom pasta. You'll go for the lamb," he said with some confidence.

"I'm getting predictable in my old age. You're probably deciding between the fish or the vegetarian option."

"I like the sound of both."

"Bat your lashes at Samuel and he'll probably let you have one of each. I'm paying enough for the damn tickets. He should be accommodating."

"Think I'll stick with the pasta." Evrain glanced around the half-full cabin. Samuel was still serving drinks.

"Probably wise. There are some great seafood places in Portland if you know where to look. Of course, it's not the same as being able to eat al fresco. Damn place is so wet."

"I enjoy the rain," Evrain said. He wasn't kidding, he loved the romanticism of wild weather.

"Well, you'll have plenty of fun in Oregon then."

"I'm looking forward to city living. It's great to have an apartment set up ready for me."

"You'll pay rent just like all the other tenants. No family favors because I own the building. It is in a nice spot, though, and I had to fight off several potential tenants to keep this unit free for you. It's fully furnished but I'm sure you'll add your own touches. Though Coryn has already been in there. He said it needed to be more 'homey and welcoming'."

"That's kind of him. If you had your way, everything would be gray and black."

"What's wrong with that?" Gregory said.

"A bit of color warms a place up, makes it cozy."

"Now you sound just like Coryn."

"It overlooks the water, doesn't it?"

"Indeed, and there's a balcony. The building is close to the Streetcar line and there's South Waterfront close by for shopping. It's a good spot—if you have to live in the land of the living damp, you should at least live there in comfort."

"I like being close to water. It's soothing somehow."

"Hmm." Gregory waved Samuel over. He took their food orders and supplied more drinks before moving smoothly away.

"Why do I get the feeling that there are certain subjects you try to avoid discussing with me?" Evrain made eye contact with his godfather and held his gaze.

"You need to learn patience, Evrain. Some things are better for the waiting. Like fine wine, some subjects must be allowed to mature before they can be fully appreciated."

Evrain sighed. "You talk in riddles."

"Have you ever thought that I might just like to cultivate an air of mystery?"

"Well, it's working. I feel like I'm on the edge of a precipice. Everything in my life is changing. New job. New country. I'm being tugged in so many directions…"

"What do you mean?"

"It's hard to describe. It's like there's a dam in my head and tiny cracks are starting to appear. I know there's going to be a flood. What I don't know is whether I'll be able to surf the wave or I'll drown in the torrent."

Gregory frowned. "You're twenty-one in three days' time, aren't you?"

"Yes. What's that got to do with anything?"

"Everything, dear boy. Everything. I promise things will become clearer, but for now just try to relax. Enjoy the flight and anticipate all the adventures that await you in your new life." Gregory closed his eyes. His mouth was set in a stubborn line.

Evrain realized he was going to get nothing further from his godfather. A vague sensation of nausea knotted his stomach, something that had been happening more and more frequently in recent months. Even as he dismissed the feeling, Evrain knew, deep down, that something was amiss. He realized that he had clenched his fingers into a tight fist and forced them to relax. He peered out of the window and watched the scudding clouds tinged with orange and red.

"Even the sky is on fire. Grandma would say it's an omen."

Gregory patted his hand. "The omens are all good, Evrain. You'll see."

* * * *

With no direct flights operating from the UK to Portland, the journey had been long and tiring even in the luxury of first class. The route had taken them from Edinburgh to Seattle and, after a short layover, from there to Portland. Almost twenty hours in total. Evrain was relieved to escape the confines of the plane and reach the bustle of the arrivals hall. He pushed a trolley loaded with his own large cases and Gregory's compact weekend bag. Needless to say the damn thing had a wonky wheel and a mind of its own. He managed to steer it across the concourse without causing actual bodily harm to other travelers but gained a bruised shin for his trouble.

Gregory, looking as fresh as if he'd just spent twenty hours at an upscale spa, strolled confidently ahead. "There's Coryn." He waved toward the crowd of people collected behind a barrier.

Evrain glanced up and spotted his second godfather. Evrain's smile was instant. Coryn had that effect on people. Tall and lean with short silver hair, he had lightly tanned skin and laughter lines that crinkled the corners of his eyes. He wore beige chinos and a chunky cream cable-knit sweater. Several women clustered around him and he seemed vaguely amused by the attention.

Gregory increased his pace. He held out his arms, and Coryn stepped into them as if they were the only place in the world he belonged. They kissed, long and slow. Evrain's temperature rose.

Fuck, those two are hot. Ugh! Why am I even thinking that?

Evidently, he wasn't the only one. A couple of wolf whistles sounded and there was the obligatory comment of, "Get a room."

When they finally separated, Coryn's eyes were glazed and dreamy, and Gregory had smug satisfaction all over his face. Evrain raised an eyebrow.

"Hi, Coryn, nice to see you."

"Evrain! How wonderful. I hope this cantankerous old miscreant hasn't caused you too much trouble on the flight over."

"Oh, I'd say he was his usual self." Evrain gave Coryn a hug. As always, Coryn's arms became a haven of safety and security. In all the times Evrain had stayed with Coryn and Gregory during his childhood, it was always Coryn who'd dealt with scraped knees, extracted splinters and removed the layers of mud that Evrain had attracted on his adventures. Coryn exuded calmness.

"Oh dear. Well, you're here now. Did you manage to get any sleep or are you exhausted? We can go straight to your place or stop for something to eat on the way."

"We got a fair amount of sleep but I've lost all track of time. What meal should we be eating?"

Coryn checked his watch. "Well, to you, it probably feels like early afternoon, but it's breakfast time. How about a big American breakfast?"

"Can I have pancakes and bacon? The bacon here is so much better than at home. I love those crispy strips." Evrain's mouth watered.

"You can have all the bacon you want. I know the perfect place." Coryn took control of the luggage trolley and guided them toward the exit.

* * * *

Two hours later, with a belly stuffed happily full, Evrain finally got to see his new home. He heaved his cases into the hall, grateful that the building had a working lift. The unit was compact but perfect for one. There was a large combination kitchen-cum-living area, and a spacious bedroom with a modern en suite. In a nook in the lounge area a full-sized tilting design table was set up under a bright light. Evrain stroked its smooth surface.

"Wow, this is top of the range."

"An early birthday present from the two of us, along with all the linens. The rest of the furniture comes with the apartment," Coryn said.

Evrain hugged Gregory and Coryn in turn. "Thank you. That's so generous and a wonderful gift." He spotted a coffee maker in the kitchen. "Please tell me there's coffee?"

"The fridge is fully stocked. I did a grocery shop for you yesterday," Coryn said. "I didn't think you'd want your first stop to be the local market, though it is a good one. Plenty of organic local produce. I got all your favorites. Well, I assume they're still your favorites, you haven't turned veggie since I last saw you, have you?"

"Still carnivorous, if white meat and fish qualifies," Evrain confirmed. "Have I ever told you how much I love you, Coryn?" He pounced on the coffee machine.

"You love that machine more," Gregory said with a grin. "We're going to give you some space. You should unpack, get some rest, explore. Your car keys are in the kitchen drawer. The car is in the parking garage underneath the building. The exit barrier has number plate recognition for residents, but there's a code if you ever have visitors over. It's a company vehicle so if it doesn't suit you, let me know. And, for goodness' sake, remember we drive on the correct side of the road over here."

"Funny, Gregory. I have driven here before. Don't you two want to stay? You've had a long journey too."

"No, thanks for the offer, though. I have a hotel booked for a few days. Very chic, with a fabulous restaurant and a spa. There's even one of those Jacuzzi baths in the suite." Coryn spoke to Evrain but winked at Gregory. Gregory grinned right back.

"We'll join you at Agatha's for your birthday and hang around to make sure you're settled before we head back to Florida." Gregory grabbed Coryn's hand. "We have some catching up to do. In the bedroom."

"Oh my God. Too much information! Go, before I'm psychologically scarred for life."

"We're out of here." Gregory towed Coryn toward the door. With a final wave, they were gone.

Enveloped in silence, Evrain took a deep breath. He strolled across to the balcony doors, pushed them open then stepped out into the fresh autumn air. Storm clouds gathered on the horizon, promising rain. Evrain rolled his shoulders in an attempt to ease the tension building at the base of his skull. His head throbbed. A sudden gust of wind ruffled his hair. The sky darkened and the air pressure felt like a physical weight on Evrain's shoulders. He couldn't wait for the coming storm to break. He took deep breaths, his head pounded. Fat drops of liquid spattered the balcony, making a pattern on the dry surface. Evrain let out his breath in a whoosh. As he exhaled a monsoon began, soaking him instantly. Evrain turned his face toward the sky, spread his arms wide and laughed. The invisible pressure around him shattered and his spirits lifted. "Welcome to America, Evrain. The past is well and truly washed away."

Chapter Two

The day of Evrain's twenty-first birthday dawned with the perfect crispy-crunch of autumn. He stood on his balcony sipping coffee, enjoying the nip in the air. The river was virtually motionless, glistening, the surface like glass. A layer of wispy mist hovered above its surface, parting here and there to allow the early morning light to catch the water in golden gleams. Evrain fancied that the atmosphere was always different on this particular day and it wasn't just because it was his birthday. On All Hallows' Eve, everything seemed full of potential. The light had a quality particular to the time of year, setting off the blaze of color in the trees perfectly. Across the river, fallen leaves carpeted the ground in ocher and amber.

Steam rose from Evrain's drink, mirroring the river. He blew gently on the surface, dissipating the heat haze. Above the river, a light breeze parted the mist. Evrain sipped his coffee and watched, intrigued, as the tendrils of fog merged once more.

Inside his apartment, the phone rang. Reluctantly, Evrain retreated inside, placed his coffee on a side table then grabbed the handset.

"Hello?"

"Sweetheart. Happy birthday! I wasn't sure you'd be up yet."

Evrain's heart warmed at the sound of his mother's voice. "Hi, Mum. How you doing?"

"Tsk. You already sound like an American. I'm perfectly well, thank you. Your father is here with me, we have you on the speaker phone thingy." Evrain's mother had never been bothered with learning about technology of any kind.

Evrain smiled. "Hey, Dad."

"Morning, son. It is morning there, isn't it? Happy birthday!"

"Stop hogging the conversation, James. My baby is twenty-one, I need to talk to him." Evrain could picture his mother elbowing his dad away from the phone.

"How come he's your baby when we're celebrating and my son when he's being rebellious?"

"Because that's the way it has worked since the beginning of time."

Evrain grinned as his parents bickered, seemingly forgetting he was on the other end of the line. He cleared his throat.

"Still here, folks."

"Oh, sorry, sweetie." His mum found her thread again. "What are you up to today? Doing anything special?"

"I'm driving out to Grandma's for lunch. Gregory and Coryn will be there too. It's a beautiful day so I'll probably take a walk while I'm out that way. There are some spectacular waterfalls not far away from the cabin."

"Sounds perfect. Give our love to everyone and you listen carefully to what your grandma has to say, okay? It's a special day."

"You're being as cryptic as she is, but I'll be on my best behavior, I promise."

"Good boy. Your sisters send their love. There should be cards in the mail if we've managed to time it right. Overseas post is so unpredictable."

"I'll look out for them, thanks."

"We weren't sure about a gift, son." Evrain's dad managed to get a word in. "I've transferred some money into your account so you can buy something you want. Make sure you use it for something special, memorable, you know?"

"I will and thanks. The gift is perfect. I'd not have been impressed if you sent me one of those awful souvenir champagne flutes."

"That's in the mail as well, son."

"Right." Evrain laughed. "I'll treasure it."

"Oh, you two!" Evrain's mum scolded them. "Enjoy your birthday, Evrain. We'll talk to you again soon." She made kissy noises down the phone.

"Bye, son." His dad stuck to simple words and no sound effects.

"Bye, thanks for calling. Give my love to everybody." Evrain replaced the receiver in its cradle. A wave of homesickness rolled over him but it was soon gone. Scotland was part of his soul and he missed his family but he was determined to make Oregon his home and make a success of his new job. He headed for the bathroom to get ready for his day out.

Evrain dressed in boots, jeans and a thick, black rollneck that was soft against his skin. He couldn't bear itchy fabrics and rarely bought anything that wasn't constructed from natural fibers. Polyester gave him hives. The Indian summer was warm enough that he didn't need a jacket. He locked up his apartment and took the lift to the basement garage. When he reached his assigned parking space, he looked around in confusion. The small blue hybrid that normally occupied his space was gone and in its place sat a gleaming red convertible. There was a note under one of the wipers. He plucked the piece of paper from beneath the blade and unfolded it.

He read the words written on it aloud. "Happy birthday, Evrain, this is yours for the day. Don't dent it! G and C." He chuckled and stroked the bonnet of the sleek machine. "Wow, it's good to be me." He searched around for keys and eventually found them under a rear wheel arch. The roof was already down, so he settled into a bucket seat that gripped his hips, holding him in place. He adjusted it to gain a bit more legroom and grasped the leather steering wheel. The ignition fired smoothly, its low purr sending gentle vibrations through his body. He put the car into gear and pulled out of his space with care. He waited until the security gate had fully risen before driving up the ramp and out into the street.

It was a perfect day for driving with the top down. Evrain knew the route from his apartment building to Hood River well. Once he was out of the city, it was simple enough to follow the I-84 east. The road followed the path of the river and it was a lovely, scenic route. Evrain concentrated on enjoying the car rather than his surroundings. He stuck to the speed limit, knowing that his flashy car would be a magnet for traffic cops. Even at a relatively sedate pace, the drive was a pleasure and Evrain was almost disappointed to reach the end of the narrow lane leading to his grandmother's cabin. He parked the car behind Coryn's rental and flipped the switch that brought the roof over. He made sure that there were no trees overhead to drop berries or so that roosting birds could use his sweet ride as target practice. He didn't want to come back to red with white polka dots rather than plain red paintwork.

He strolled along the lane to his grandmother's place, Hornbeam Cottage, his feet crunching in the fallen leaves. As a child he had loved to gather piles of leaves in the woods near his home in the Highlands and jump in them. He and his sisters had spent many happy autumn days doing just that, then gathering shiny conkers. He used to soak his in vinegar to harden them. Threaded on old shoelaces, they became effective weapons and he'd suffered many a bruised knuckle at school in drawn-out conker tournaments.

He whistled as he walked. The breeze whipped the leaves into eddies around his ankles. Evrain glanced at the sky through the trees, wondering if the strengthening wind was a sign of rain. He had no coat and didn't want to get caught in a sudden storm. Where before there had been patches of blue, the sky was now a bruised purple. Evrain hurried along, breaking into a jog. As he reached Agatha's porch, sure enough the heavens opened. He shoved open the door, which she never locked, avoiding the first heavy drops by seconds.

"What's with the weather today?" Evrain exclaimed, as his grandmother and godfathers turned toward him from their seats around the fire. "I swear I left Portland in the most glorious sunshine but I seem to have dragged a storm along with me."

Coryn and Gregory exchanged glances. Agatha rose from her chair and came toward him, holding out her arms.

"Give your old grandma a hug, birthday boy."

Evrain bent to accept Agatha's embrace. He kissed the top of her head. She smelled of nutmeg and ginger, the scent familiar and comforting.

"Happy birthday, Evrain."

"Thank you, Grandma."

Coryn and Gregory queued to take their turns for hugs.

"Did you enjoy the drive over?" Coryn asked, his eyes twinkling.

"I did. Thank you both, so much. It was a great gift and a brilliant surprise. I could get used to driving around in that."

"Sorry to disappoint you, but it's just for the day. A special treat."

Evrain shrugged. "I'll take it." He cast his gaze at each of the people he loved. They returned his scrutiny with an intensity that made him feel a little uncomfortable. "What? Do I have a smudge on my nose or something?" He walked over to the fire and peered into the mirror hanging over the mantel. As far as he could tell there were no weird marks or splotches.

"How are you feeling? Any unexplained headaches or nausea recently?" Gregory asked.

"No. My joints are a bit sore but I'm putting that down to a lack of exercise over the last few days. I was going to hike along the river this afternoon and shake off some of the lethargy. I haven't been sleeping well—

I think I'm still getting adjusted to the time zone." Evrain's sense of discomfort grew. It wasn't like Gregory to ask after his health. "Why the sudden interest in whether or not I have the sniffles? Is there a weird hereditary disease in the family that I don't know about?"

"Why don't you take a seat by the fire? There's something we need to talk to you about."

"Is this some kind of intervention?" Now he was really worried. "I've heard about those. I promise I'm not a drunk, I don't take drugs and I'm not addicted to gambling." He gave a nervous laugh.

Gregory stood. He placed his hand on Evrain's shoulder and squeezed. "It's nothing to worry about. In fact, it should make things a whole lot clearer for you. I think it's time. Agatha?"

"Indeed. The hour doesn't matter. I geared everything to the date." She hummed a strange tune under her breath.

"And a very significant date it is." Gregory guided him to a chair, ignoring Agatha's weird behavior.

Evrain sat, sinking into the overstuffed cushion. He'd need a cleaver to cut the atmosphere, not just a knife. Or maybe a scythe, that seemed appropriate. Agatha's gothic mantel clock began to chime. Evrain's senses sharpened. He could pick out every detail, every thread of the woven hearth rug. A mixture of intense aromas — spices, burning wood, candle wax, even Gregory's aftershave — assaulted his nose. He wanted to cover his ears there was so much sound — spitting and crackling from the fire, leaves and branches thrashing outside in the wind, breathing, heartbeats. Evrain gasped. It was too much. He gripped the arms of his chair and felt every imperfection in the wood. His head swam.

"What's... What's happening?" He squeezed the words from between gritted teeth.

In the hearth, the fire exploded, sending huge flames shooting up the chimney. The storm outside intensified, pounding at the cabin with weapons of hail and wind. Evrain took short, sharp breaths. He sensed movement behind him and swiveled around to see the pot plants on the windowsill sprouting shoots and new leaves at incredible speed, the foliage spilling over countertops and onto the floor. This could not be happening. The pressure in his head built to an intolerable level. He was aware of Gregory's touch, clasping his hand.

"Let it go, Evrain. Don't be afraid." Gregory's voice, calm and soothing, penetrated his panic.

Evrain willed his body to relax. Multicolored lights exploded before his eyes, then everything went mercifully dark.

* * * *

"Evrain, you're a warlock."

"What the hell happened, Grandma? Am I ill? My head feels like a grenade exploded. Inside it." Evrain massaged his temples and groaned. "Wait. What did you just say?"

"I said, my dear boy, that *you* are a warlock. Now drink this, it will make you feel better. You were out cold for a few minutes there." She thrust a mug into his trembling hands.

"What is it?" He sniffed the drink with some suspicion.

"Butterbur, chamomile and ginger root tea sweetened with a little honey. My own remedy and better than any chemical you could poison your body with."

"Does it cure insanity, because I could have sworn that you just told me I'm a warlock?"

"It doesn't, and you are. Don't be a child. Drink it."

"Don't be a— Gregory! Please tell me I'm hearing things." He looked to his godfather who stood in front of the fire making strange movements with his fingers.

"Just hold on a minute, Evrain. I need to damp down your conflagration a little."

"What? Wait... You're... Oh my God. I'm in an alternate reality, aren't I?" He addressed his question to Coryn, sitting in the chair next to him. Coryn seemed a bit pale despite the heat. His smile was full of sympathy and understanding.

"It's true, Evrain. You *are* a warlock and so is Gregory. Your grandma put a suppression spell on your powers shortly after you were born, to protect you. You heard her humming? Well, she was lifting the spell. You have come into your powers. You're very strong, Evrain. The change was too much for you and you blacked out for a few minutes." He paused as Gregory came and stood next to him.

"You okay, love?" Gregory asked Coryn, stroking his face.

"Sure." Coryn lifted his face for a kiss. "He takes some containing, doesn't he?"

"He does. Evrain, I know this is difficult for you to take in, to understand, but deep down I think you've always known that you were different. The elements have always behaved strangely around you, haven't they? Weird weather, unpredictable flames, thriving plants… You are so strong that your power occasionally leaked through the barrier spell."

Evrain examined his hands. "I feel strange. Under pressure. I don't mean stress, I mean literal, physical pressure. Like a saucepan full of boiling water with the lid on too tight. Does that make any sense?"

"You need to release some energy or the headache will return. It's something you'll have to do every day if you want to stay healthy. I'm here to teach you how to do it safely. We wouldn't want half the state disappearing down a chasm in the ground or going up in flames, now, would we?"

"Um, no?"

"No."

"Wait. Do my parents know about this? Am I the only one who's been kept in ignorance?"

Gregory took Evrain's mug and replaced it with a glass of sloe gin, which he chugged back in one go. The liquid burned all the way to his gut.

"Lyssa and James understand that you have certain…gifts. That knowledge has influenced their decisions about your childhood. They don't need to know anything further — indeed, for their own safety it's better they don't." Gregory rolled his shoulders. "Agatha is, of course, a witch. In your family line there have been many witches over the centuries. You, however, are something of an anomaly. Agatha has a wonderful birthday meal prepared for you. You can ask all the questions you wish about your family history while we eat. Once the sun has gone down, I'll teach you a method for dispersing your power."

Evrain looked around for more gin. "I shouldn't believe a word of this. It's totally barmy."

Coryn filled his glass and left the decanter on a side table within Evrain's reach.

"But you do, don't you?" Gregory stated. "You know it's true."

"Yes. I do." Evrain sighed. "I am so fucked."

"Language, Evrain!" Agatha cuffed his head.

"Sorry, Grandma. Will you turn me into a frog for swearing?"

Agatha cuffed him again. "Cheeky boy. It does nobody any good to perpetuate silly myths like that. I don't own a pointy hat or a wand, nor do I have a familiar. Try to avoid regressing into a plotline from *Harry Potter*."

"Yes, ma'am." Evrain rubbed his head.

Gregory sniggered.

"Why don't we eat?" Coryn said.

"Ever the peacemaker, darling. But that's a fine idea. Don't worry, Evrain, there's no eye of bat or leg of toad on the menu." Gregory chuckled.

"Shouldn't that be... Oh, never mind, I can't believe I'm even thinking about getting into a debate on the subject of potion ingredients."

"Why don't we let Coryn and Agatha get everything ready while we go outside and deal with your little problem? I don't think we can wait until darkness. You might burst and that would be messy."

"Oh my God, I won't, will I?" Evrain prodded his flat stomach. There was no sign of inflation.

"You know, if you say gullible really slowly, it sounds like chicken," Gregory said.

"That's just mean. Feeling vulnerable here!"

Everybody laughed. Evrain knocked back another sloe gin before he risked getting to his feet and even then he wobbled. Gregory put an arm around his shoulders and led him outside.

The rain still pounded down, beating the earth to mud. Evrain turned his face to the stormy sky and let the drops batter his skin. Some of his tension eased.

"You and I are elemental warlocks, Evrain," Gregory declared. "That means we have an affinity with air, earth, fire and water. My power is linked most strongly to water, which is one of the reasons I settled in Florida. Plenty of the stuff there and it's not constantly falling out of the sky like it is here. In time, you'll discover which element attracts you most. The power is always in you, but it can build, particularly when your emotions are heightened. So every now and again, we need to release the pressure valve. It's termed 'venting'. Don't ask me where that comes from because I've no idea, but it fits."

"Show me, Gregory. I feel like a firework about to go off." Evrain rolled up his shirtsleeves, craving more cool rain on his overheated skin.

"It's not difficult. You're primed and ready, but the first time can take a while. It seems dramatic but holding out your arms helps." Gregory stood in the open, his arms spread. He turned his hands so that the palms were up, then touched the second and fourth fingers of each hand together at the tip.

"Clear your thoughts, then get an image of release in your mind. I use Old Faithful, but anything will do." He closed his eyes and seconds later light shot from his fingers into the sky. He gave a happy sigh. "Your turn."

Evrain mirrored his stance and closed his eyes. He fixed an image in his mind. Heat penetrated the soles of his feet as if he stood on molten lava. The burn spread through his body, fire in his veins. As it reached his fingertips, his head jerked back and he screamed. All the pressure in his body left in a rush, the sensation dropping him to his knees. He opened his eyes, checking his hands for scorch marks, but there were none.

"Did it work, Gregory? I feel much better. Lighter." He got to his feet.

Gregory was staring off into the distance.

"Gregory?"

Gregory pointed. Evrain followed the direction of Gregory's finger and gaped.

"Oh."

"Hmm. That's one way of putting it. I think you may need to make sure you're pointing at the sky in future." Three huge conifers had been reduced to smoking stumps. "What the hell were you thinking of?"

"I couldn't decide between Mt. St. Helens going up or Vesuvius decimating Pompeii, so I kind of lined them up next to each other in my head and added Krakatoa for luck."

"Good Lord, boy, you don't mess about." Gregory sniggered.

"It felt like my entire body was on fire, but I had no idea..." Evrain stared at the damage he'd done. "What the hell am I?"

Gregory put his arm around Evrain's shoulders. "Probably the most powerful warlock in a thousand years. Let's eat." Gregory guided him toward the house.

Evrain laughed. It was that or cry. "Happy birthday to me. I'd say this day is going to be one of the more memorable in my life so far."

"Definitely one for the family album," Gregory said. "I'm sure there will be plenty more to come."

Evrain looked back over his shoulder at the destruction he'd caused. "Just so long as they don't include jail time or a stint in the local asylum."

Chapter Three

"Evrain, if you don't sit still and concentrate, I swear on our lady moon, I will make sure you regret it." Agatha stamped her foot, her frustration all too evident. "You have to apply yourself. Practice makes perfect."

Evrain, sitting at Agatha's well-scrubbed kitchen table, scowled. "You think I don't know that?"

"I swear, Evrain, if you weren't my grandson..." Agatha narrowed her eyes and treated him to a glare capable of withering thistles at the root.

Evrain swallowed nervously. His grandmother never made empty threats and he'd been on the receiving end of her harsh discipline too many times in the last few months to risk further punishment. She might look like a sweet old lady but Agatha was frighteningly creative when it came to making his life difficult. She was the one person he respected enough to back down when his impatience and frustration threatened to get the best of him. Compliance wasn't in his nature, something all too apparent in the sometimes fiery relationship he maintained with his father. Agatha was ten times scarier than his dad, even on his worst day. Evrain pushed back a smile. He and his dad might fight but the love between them was just as fierce. He missed him. Not that he would admit that in a million years.

"Sorry, Grandmother." Evrain's tone was sweet enough to be decorated with candy flowers and hearts. That got him another hard stare.

"Sarcasm is unbecoming in one so young and untried. Perhaps in fifty years or so, when you have finally managed to absorb what I'm trying to teach you, then I might grant you a little latitude. But not now. Do I have to call your godfather Gregory again?"

"No! No, Grandma. I'll behave." Evrain batted his lashes shamelessly. He resisted the urge to point out that in fifty years' time Agatha would be breaking world records in the age department. She might be a tough old bird but she was still his grandma and therefore susceptible to his dark, spaniel eyes. The last thing Evrain needed was to be tag-teamed by Agatha and his godfather. Separately they were formidable. Together. Evrain shuddered at the thought.

He shifted his chair back a little, twisted his fingers into the required shape and pushed his thoughts at the fat, white candle in front of him. The tingle that shot down his spine could have preceded an orgasm. *If only!* There was a whoosh of heat as the flame shot toward the ceiling and the candle became no more than a spattered puddle of melted wax spreading across the table. Evrain yelped and blew on his singed fingers in an attempt to cool the scorch marks. He scowled again.

"Take that look off your face, young man." Agatha was pitiless. She scraped at the cooling wax with a brightly painted nail. "Once this has cooled, you can lift it all off the wood. With a toothpick. That will give you some time to meditate."

Evrain groaned. "Grandma, this is hopeless. I'm not getting any better, just more and more destructive. If I keep going like this, you'll need to have the fire service on standby for when the cabin goes up in flames."

"Nonsense. You're like all young people these days — you want everything easy. The craft takes time, patience and perseverance. You would do well to remember that," Agatha scolded.

"Mind you... A bunch of firemen hanging around does have some appeal."

Agatha rolled her eyes. "You are a very bad boy. Less daydreaming about men and more application to your studies, please." She sighed. "That's enough for today. Put the kettle on and make your old grandma a cup of primrose tea. Then you have a table to clean."

Agatha watched Evrain as he moved with effortless grace around her kitchen. His aura flickered and sparked. The colors had mellowed as he'd matured, changing from aluminum foil silver and gold leaf to warm copper and platinum swirls. The energy around him burned hot. Agatha worried constantly about his need to channel some of his power. Evrain was restless, unfocused. His abilities manifested in intense creativity and extreme emotion. Even though he vented almost every day, he still needed a calming influence in his life, and soon.

Evrain set a burnished copper kettle on the range. He flicked his fingers and steam immediately issued from the spout. The kettle rocked and shook as its contents boiled with unusual violence. Evrain gave Agatha a sheepish glance. "Sorry?"

"Why are you turning an apology into a question, young man? You shouldn't have done that and you know it… Especially after what happened last time."

Evrain peered up at the ceiling. "There's hardly a mark."

Agatha shook her head. Kitchen paraphernalia exploding into the air was a minor annoyance in the scheme of things. She shifted in her chair, settling into a more comfortable position. "Do you realize it's been six months to the day since you turned twenty-one?"

Evrain poured steaming water into two mugs and spooned in aromatic herbs. "Six months to the day since you turned my world upside down." He brought the drinks across to the table. "Let it steep for a few minutes." He took the chair across from Agatha. "I still can't believe your opening line was 'Evrain, you're a warlock.' Subtle, Grandma."

"Your expression was a picture."

"You gave me no time to think, just launched into seven hundred years of family history over what was supposed to be my birthday lunch."

Agatha's thoughts drifted back to that late autumn day. They'd enjoyed a pleasant meal together then had settled in the armchairs next to the open fire with a glass or two of home-brewed sloe gin. Without preamble she had told Evrain of his heritage, Gregory and Coryn chiming in now and again. There had been no softening of the news. Evrain had to be strong to cope with his abilities and the training entailed in learning to control them.

"Virtually every generation of our family has sired a witch, though your mother did not inherit the gift. You are a great rarity."

Evrain sighed. "I don't feel special... I feel... I don't even know how to explain it. Disconnected. That's as close as I can get. I have this strange sense that I'm being pulled in several directions at once and I don't know which way to go."

"To varying degrees witches and warlocks are linked to the elements, some more strongly than others. For witches, the Earth's pull is by far the strongest." She held him with her gaze. "You are a true elemental warlock – all four powers seem to call to you equally at the moment, though you might still find a stronger link to one. Fire maybe." She rolled her eyes. "It was obvious, even while you were growing up. I suppressed your abilities until you were old enough to cope with the pressure, but you are so strong that you started fighting the block without even knowing it. Your mother noticed, of course, and it was crystal clear to your godfather and me whenever you came to stay in the holidays. Whenever your emotions were heightened, tiny indications of what you might become began to manifest themselves. Fires burned brighter around you, storms became wilder, streams surged faster – the evidence of your link to the elements was plain to see for anyone who knew what to look for."

Evrain wrapped slim fingers around his mug and hunched his shoulders. "Will it ever get any easier?"

"You have a great deal of learning ahead of you. You know that. This isn't an easy life, Evrain. Very few people know that warlocks exist, but among them there are those that would harm you. Those that would seek to manipulate you or use your abilities for their own ends. Gregory and I will teach you as much as we can, especially how to defend yourself, but you must be careful to keep your talents secret."

"I know. Believe me, I do not want to end up committed to the funny farm. You had to tell Grandpa, though, and Gregory told Coryn."

Agatha placed her mug carefully on the hearth. "Perhaps it's time…"

"Time for what?" Evrain asked. "There can't be any family secrets left that are worse than what you've already told me." He gave her a sharp look. "Can there?"

"Every day your strength increases. It's finesse you lack, but despite what I've been telling you, that doesn't just come from practice. Not for a warlock. You need balance, a calming influence through which some of your immense power can dissipate. It's called channeling."

Evrain frowned. "I don't understand."

"How can I explain?" Agatha leaned back in her chair. "Coryn isn't just Gregory's husband—he is a conduit for Gregory's energy. A channeler. When Gregory uses his power, his deep emotional link with Coryn allows some of that power to filter through Coryn's body. Think of it like power generation. You've seen how a substation sparks in a storm, yet electricity through wire is safe and controlled. Gregory is the power station."

"And Coryn is the wire?"

"Yes."

"So was Grandpa a channeler for you?"

"No, witches don't need to channel, our power is nowhere near wild enough. But all warlocks need someone. It's not easy to find the right person either.

Channeling for a warlock hurts. It requires a relationship founded on the deepest love and trust, and that in itself is hard to find."

"So what you're saying is that until I find a partner prepared to channel for me, my power will remain unpredictable?"

"I'm afraid so. It's not something you need to worry about yet, but without a means to channel, the wild magic can overcome you. Subsume you, until you no longer wish to control it."

Agatha observed the emotions flashing through Evrain's eyes. Anger, fear, a touch of hope. Beside them the fire roared, flames shooting up the chimney as if someone had dumped kerosene on them.

"What man is ever going to want me if it means a lifetime of pain?" Evrain asked. "And if I never find someone, what then? Wild magic let loose can't be a good thing."

"Just like Gregory found Coryn, there is someone out there for you, Evrain. He'll probably be where you least expect him."

Evrain's eyes narrowed. "There's something else you're not telling me, Grandma."

"Not at all," she denied it with a smile. "Now, it's been a long day. Go home. You will need to have studied the next chapter of the grimoire by tomorrow evening."

Her grandson stood and looked down on her from his full six feet and two inches. Dark green eyes flecked with gold regarded her with a frightening intensity until black lashes blinked and he smiled. For a moment Agatha saw herself in the sharp features and raven-black hair. She insisted that he should be neat, clean-shaven with tidy hair. He grudgingly complied, accepting her justification that discipline in his personal life would filter through to his mastery of the craft. Only the slight hollows beneath his eyes shadowed his pale, smooth skin.

"No one else is allowed to speak to me as you do, Grandmother."

Evrain's voice was unexpectedly quiet but authoritative, and Agatha knew that only his understanding of what she was trying to do ensured his obedience. Evrain was self-assured and confident in most things, but this aspect of his life was still uncharted territory.

He bent and kissed the top of her head. "I'll see you tomorrow."

"And get some proper sleep, boy. You have a lot of hard work ahead of you and I can tell you're tired. No partying."

He grinned. "No burning the candle at both ends, huh?"

"Candles everywhere just quaked in fear. Get out of here."

"Yes, ma'am."

"Oh, Evrain?"

"Yes?"

"Don't think I've forgotten that table. The wax will be waiting for you tomorrow."

He was out of the door before she could cuff him for his cheeky tone. Agatha watched through the small kitchen window as Evrain strolled down the garden path and out of the gate, shutting it carefully behind him. He moved with the ease of youth, and just for a moment Agatha regretted the passing of the years. True, her talents allowed her to stay healthy and few would credit her with the seventy-five years since her birth, but she was beginning to feel tired, her bones ached. Her driving need to ensure Evrain's future kept her going but she looked forward to a time when she could relax in the knowledge that he was safe.

Chapter Four

Dominic Castine straightened his slim frame and rubbed his lower back with a groan. Much as he loved his gardening business, sometimes it could be backbreaking work. It certainly kept him fit — he had no need of an expensive gym membership — but sometimes the aches built up enough that there was certainly some appeal in the thought of a sauna or steam room. "I'll just have to make do with a hot bath," he muttered. He took a step back and ran a muddy hand through sweat-dampened hair, taking a critical look at the herb bed he had been planting.

"It looks perfect, Dominic."

Agatha's voice at Dominic's shoulder made him jump. He would never get used to the fact that she could sneak up on him so silently but he turned and smiled down at her diminutive frame. He stood almost a foot taller than her stooped five feet nothing but she still managed to make him feel like a little boy, eager to please.

"Thanks, Aggie. There are one or two plants that I haven't managed to get hold of yet but I should have them by the end of the week. It's coming together nicely, though. Should keep you well stocked with herbs for your medicines once everything takes hold. The ground here is so fertile I'm sure everything will thrive."

"The earth works hard for your green fingers," Aggie said. "The light will be going soon. Why don't you come inside and have something to drink. I've also got some balm that you can take home with you to rub on your back."

"How did you...? Never mind." Dominic was sure Agatha hadn't been there when he'd first stood up so how did she know his back was sore? She always seemed to know about his aches and pains, how he was feeling or if something was bothering him. He had decided long ago not to question her intuition. He suspected that she practiced some form of witchcraft, but whatever she did it was certainly benign and he'd never had cause to think that she meant him any harm. Quite the opposite in fact.

He followed her back toward the kitchen, stopping on the way to use cold water from the outside tap to wash some of the sweat and grime from his face and hands. He removed his heavy work boots, left them under the porch where they wouldn't get wet if it rained, then went inside. In his thick woolen socks, he padded across to the kitchen area of the open plan room and sat in his usual spot at the table. A small bouquet of wildflowers nestled in a jelly jar was positioned in the center of the table. He recognized autumn crocuses and hebe among the blooms. The scent rose to tickle his nostrils. The warmth of the room wrapped around him like a hug.

"Something smells good, Aggie. What are you cooking?" Savory aromas drifted from the range, overwhelming the sweeter scent of the flowers.

"Vegetable stew, with some of your herbs of course. It does smell good." She rubbed her stomach and grinned. "It'll be ready in half an hour or so. There's plenty if you want to stay."

She didn't push the invitation, and Dominic was grateful. Agatha never pressured him into anything or made him feel guilty for preferring his own company on occasion. He disliked making decisions unless it concerned where to plant a particular shrub or when to cut back a fruit tree. People were complicated. Dominic preferred clear instructions and loved the sense of satisfaction he got from meeting expectations. Social situations were a challenge even with someone as easygoing as Agatha.

He never charged Agatha for the work he did on her large garden. In exchange for his hard labor, she taught him about the many uses for herbs and plants. Her knowledge was extensive and she was a mine of information about natural pest control and the best way to encourage plants to flourish in difficult conditions. It was an arrangement that suited them both, and Dominic genuinely enjoyed her company.

Cupping his mug with fingers engrained with mud despite his attempts to clean them, Dominic listened intently to Agatha's latest lecture on the medicinal properties of sage.

"Let's see if you've been paying attention, shall we?" She sounded like a particularly stern junior high-school teacher Dominic had once been taught by. "Which herb family does sage come from?"

"The mint family. I don't know the Latin name," Dominic said.

"And which other herbs come from that family?"

"Oregano, lavender, rosemary, thyme and basil," he recited, happy that he remembered.

"Very good. Now, can you describe sage for me?"

"Gray-green leaves and blue or purple flowers?" He thought he recalled other varieties.

"Yes, the flowers can be white or pink as well, though. What about some uses?"

"There are quite a lot. It has antiseptic and anti-inflammatory properties and it's supposed to be good for digestive problems."

"Very good. There's also been some research into it improving memory and, though this won't be of much interest to you, it's good for controlling hot flushes in women of a certain age."

Dominic chuckled.

"It also tastes damn good in stew!" Agatha got up to stir the pot on the stove.

Dominic relaxed in his chair and gazed around the cozy kitchen. Aggie's cabin had become a second home to him in recent months. There was something about the old building that felt safe. Crazy really because Aggie rarely locked her doors. The décor was a mishmash of colors and styles that suited Aggie perfectly. Most of the furniture was reclaimed or gifted from people who'd benefited from Aggie's home remedies. The walls were adorned with tapestry work, delicate watercolors and detailed oils that glowed with jewel-like colors. Bunches of drying herbs hung from hooks above the window.

"I wonder why they ran electricity out here, it's pretty remote." Dominic eyed the expensive coffee maker on the kitchen counter. He'd never seen Aggie drink coffee the whole time he'd known her. She was strictly a herbal tea girl.

"My powers of persuasion are world-renowned. Forty years ago there were state grants to connect more remote properties to the grid if you knew where to go. I have a few connections. I like my home comforts. What would I do without my nature documentaries and current affairs programs?"

"You mean soap operas and thrillers, don't you?" Dominic knew full well that Agatha was addicted to some daily shows. He'd been forced to sit through a couple of them.

Aggie cackled. "You know me too well."

"I've also detected a theme of gratuitous shirtlessness."

"I'm old, not dead. Besides, I didn't see you looking away."

Dominic's cheeks heated. He hoped the blushing could be put down to the warmth of the open fire.

The light had faded completely and Dominic had started to think about the walk back to his truck. It was far enough to be unpleasant in the cold, and if it rained, it would be downright miserable. He was warm and comfortable so he wasn't in any rush to venture out. A sharp knocking interrupted his procrastination. The door swung inward with some violence, banging against the wall. A stunning young man, not much older than Dominic, lugging two large paper sacks of groceries, collapsed through the door. Dominic stared in shock. He realized the newcomer must be Aggie's grandson, Evrain. She'd talked about him a lot and

Dominic almost felt like he knew him already, even though they had never met. Her description didn't do Evrain justice—he was absolutely gorgeous. Dominic's temperature rose even further. The fact that his cock was swelling rapidly didn't help. He clamped his gaping mouth shut but couldn't look away.

"Some help would be nice, or are you just going to sit there and stare?" Evrain snapped.

It took Dominic a few seconds to realize that Evrain had directed the comment at him, and was now glaring at him with the most beautiful dark green eyes Dominic had ever seen. Evrain elbowed the door shut behind him. Belatedly, Dominic pushed his chair back, crossed the kitchen with rapid strides and held out his arms for the bags. Evrain shoved them both into Dominic's grasp with a sigh of relief.

"That fucking lane gets longer every time I walk down it." Evrain shrugged off his jacket, slung it around the back of Dominic's recently vacated seat then sat heavily, claiming the spot for himself.

"Language, Evrain." Agatha handed him a mug of tea, then bent to receive a kiss on her cheek. "If you want coffee instead, you can grapple with that demonic machine yourself." She gestured at the shiny chrome coffee maker.

Evrain sipped from his mug. "This is fine, thanks. It's a chilly evening. I need warming up." He looked directly at Dominic as he spoke.

"Dominic, allow me to introduce you to my impudent grandson, Evrain Brookes."

Dominic swallowed. He was dealing with the thoughts of what warming up Evrain might entail. He pushed the bulging shopping bags onto the kitchen counter.

"Nice to meet you." Dominic didn't look at Evrain, just muttered the greeting under his breath and edged toward the door. In the presence of this charismatic man, Dominic's fight or flight instincts lurched toward escape with the subtlety of a stampeding herd of wildebeest. There was no doubt in his mind that Evrain was a predator on the hunt.

"Going so soon?" Evrain smirked and raised a dark eyebrow.

"I should... I mean... I don't..."

"You're very welcome to stay for some supper," Aggie said, rescuing him from his tongue-tied misery and renewing her invitation. "There's plenty to go round."

"Thanks, Aggie, but—" He took a steadying breath. "I should be going." Dominic was halfway out of the door and pulling on his boots in the storm porch before she could stop him. Aggie stood by the stove, hands on hips, ladle in her hand. She glanced from Dominic to Evrain then back again.

"Another time then." She sounded amused rather than disappointed.

Dominic peered past her and met a very intimidating gaze. Evrain's strange eyes seemed to pierce his soul.

"Yes, of course. Another time. That would be great." He pulled the door closed behind him, cutting off Aggie's response.

"Evrain, you scared him!" Agatha latched the door, which had banged open again after Dominic's hasty exit. She swiveled toward the table where Evrain was playing thoughtfully with his mug and didn't seem to hear her. Agatha nodded. She grabbed a candle from the shelf above the stove and deposited it on the table in front of Evrain. "Light it," she said quietly.

Evrain moved his fingers automatically. The wick ignited with a soft pop and a delicate flame flickered happily.

"I thought as much." Agatha plopped down on another chair and smiled. "Tell me what you were thinking about when you did that."

Evrain blinked. "I don't think that would be such a good idea, Grandma."

"Don't be coy. Perhaps I should have asked *who* you were thinking about rather than *what*."

"I don't know what you mean," Evrain replied, his tone stubborn.

"You were thinking about *him*, weren't you?"

"Who?"

Agatha hissed. "You were thinking about Dominic. Your emotional energy was channeled toward him, allowing you to control your power and light the candle without the usual pyrotechnics. You're attracted to him, aren't you?"

"Even if I was, Grandma, I'd hardly confess it to you! And we just met." Evrain's pale skin flushed slightly.

"Why not? I know all your secrets. Who was it you first came out to?"

"You, but that doesn't count since you knew before I did that I was gay."

"That's because there's never been a warlock born who wasn't." Agatha rolled her eyes. "You were never going to be the exception to that rule."

Evrain grinned. "True. But can we get off the extremely uncomfortable topic of my sex life and eat? I'm starving."

Agatha ladled the stew into big, earthenware bowls. She put them on the table along with a crusty loaf and a carving knife. Evrain immediately sawed off a huge chunk of the bread.

"You baked! I love you." He slathered the bread with butter and took an enormous bite. He groaned. "So good!"

Agatha took her seat and sampled a small mouthful of the stew. She hummed her appreciation. "This *is* delicious — flavored with herbs that Dominic grew in my garden."

"It's excellent." Evrain didn't take the bait. "One of your best, in fact."

"He's very shy you know. Painfully so. It's taken me months to get him comfortable here and now you've frightened him away."

Clearly Evrain's attempt to alter the course of the conversation had not succeeded. "Well, I'll apologize next time I see him. Not that I did anything wrong. How was I to know he was more skittish than a newborn foal?"

"You use your senses, boy. Or does a pretty face completely destroy your ability to read an expression, to interpret body language?"

Evrain chewed his bread thoughtfully. "He is exceptionally pretty."

Agatha chuckled. "He's one of the best-looking boys I've ever come across. I could imagine him smiling from the pages of one of those fashion magazines you read, or acting on the television."

"I don't read fashions magazines, Grandma. Lifestyle ones occasionally. And if he is as shy as you say, he'd hate it. He probably wouldn't be able to imagine anything worse than being in the spotlight that way. Celebrity is just shallow nonsense anyway."

"He is intensely private. He started working on the garden a year ago and I've still only managed to squeeze just a few small pieces of personal information out of him."

"How did you find him, Grandma? You've never said." Evrain fetched the stew pan from the stove and served himself another helping.

"Well, at the time I was looking to rescue the kitchen garden. It has become sadly neglected since your grandfather passed. It was always his thing more than mine. I asked at the plant center in town if they knew of anyone trustworthy, and the manager there gave me Dominic's name. He started his business when he was just eighteen with a small grant and it flourished just like plants do under his hands. He's a talented gardener but willing to take on any job, however small or menial, which gives him an advantage over larger local firms. He works long hours, he works hard and he's scrupulously honest — a rare combination. Once I asked around a few people, it became apparent that he had more work than he could cope with. I didn't think he'd have time for me at all."

"So how did you acquire his services? He's done a huge amount of work on your garden."

"You noticed!"

"Of course I did. It was like *The Day of the Triffids* out there. I needed a machete to get up the path before he started working on it."

"Cheeky boy. I asked him to come over and take a look. He showed up one Sunday and fell in love with the place. We agreed a trade-off. I provide the land. He supplies hard labor and puts up with me lecturing him about herb-lore. Anything he grows he can use in his business, once he's supplied my needs. The herb garden is almost finished and he's already planted the vegetable patch he's dug in. I'm hoping for flowers and fruit trees next."

"He had mud in his hair," Evrain murmured. "That dark red is so unusual."

"It needs a cut. He's been saying so for weeks. The longer it gets, the wavier it becomes. It flops into his eyes then he brushes it away with mucky hands while he's working. It's always full of dirt, stalks and leaves."

"I'll bet his hands are rough." Evrain examined his own soft palms. The only callous he had was from holding a pen. "But his skin was the color of fresh cream. How does he manage to avoid getting tan? He just had a light dusting of freckles across the bridge of his nose. I'd have thought the ravages of the weather would have been unavoidable in his job."

"With his coloring, he burns easily so he wears a hat and plenty of sunscreen. You noticed an awful lot about him from such a short meeting."

Evrain gave her a sharp look. "How long have you been trying to get us in the same place, Grandma?"

"He has the prettiest blue eyes too. A perfect contrast to his lashes, which are just a shade darker than his hair."

"Grandma..." Evrain's voice rumbled low with warning.

"He's intelligent too, and curious. He may not have had your expensive education, but Dominic has a sharp mind."

Evrain pushed his chair back and moved to stand behind Agatha. He massaged her shoulders gently, and she moaned with pleasure.

"You're incorrigible. My own grandmother trying to set me up. Still, I don't think it's going to happen. If I were his type, he would have stayed to eat. Is he even gay? Oh my God, you didn't ask him that, did you?"

"Yes, he's gay, and how I know is none of your business. Dominic's an innocent compared to you. I don't think he knows what he wants yet. It's up to you to show him what you have to offer."

Evrain walked across to the fire and stared into the flames. "And what's that? I doubt a warlock is that high on his list of potential boyfriends."

"Oh, Evrain. Have a little faith. Court him gently."

"This is not the 1940s, Grandma."

"You could learn some manners. Curb that assertiveness. Wine and dine him some. He has an apartment above the diner in town. I promised him some ointment for his back but he left so quickly he forgot to take it. You can take it with you and call on him."

"Considering that there was barely repressed panic all over his face from one brief meeting, I'm not sure that showing up at his door is going to go down all that well."

Agatha pressed a small tin into his hand with a knowing smile. "You won't know until you try, now, will you?"

Chapter Five

Hornbeam Cottage sat on the very edge of Hood River, clinging to the vestiges of civilization while reaching for the wilderness. Dominic could stand in the garden and feel like he had a foot in both camps. He fancied that the structure, built almost entirely from locally sourced natural materials, had its heart firmly fixed in the wild. He may have begun to tame the extensive gardens but around the borders nature constantly fought back. If he looked away, Gaia's fingers went to work claiming back the fertile soil.

Part of the reason the place felt so remote was the lack of access for vehicles. When he drove, Dominic had to park his van almost a quarter of a mile away where the tarmac ended, then follow the narrow track that led to Agatha's rickety gate. Trees bent over the track, reaching for one another, forming a leafy tunnel. Dominic imagined himself as a character in a fairy tale as he walked its length, sunlight dappling the ground. When it rained, as it did often, the pleasant stroll became a muddy slog and the real world impinged on his daydreams.

Tonight, he was thankful that the rain held off. After retreating from Agatha's hospitality with unseemly haste, bordering on rudeness, he half jogged along the track. Part of the way back to civilization, he stopped and bent over, hands braced on his thighs, gasping for air. He'd been holding his breath without even realizing it. His heart was pounding and a sensation of mild panic urged him to run. Agatha was a little kooky and she definitely dabbled in things Dominic chose not to ask questions about, but she'd never given him cause to be afraid. Her cabin had an air of calm benevolence about it that he loved — but tonight that had changed.

The wooded lane seemed unusually quiet. Around him the leaves rustled in the breeze, but that was it. No birdsong, no small mammals scurrying through the undergrowth, just an eerie silence and the wind ruffling his hair. Dominic took a couple of cleansing deep breaths. He closed his eyes and all he could see was Evrain Brookes' handsome face. Dominic shook his head but the image didn't shift. Glossy black hair, pale skin and those weirdly magnetic green eyes haunted him. Evrain's looks were striking but there was something else about him that called to Dominic, a siren call of assertive confidence. Seeing him sat in Aggie's kitchen chair, long legs outstretched, slender fingers gripping his mug, Dominic had felt the urge to drop to his knees at the man's feet.

"Shit, shit, shit, what the hell's wrong with me?" He continued at a steadier pace and soon covered the remainder of the distance to his truck. It was a relief to reach the enclosed space of the cab. He clambered inside, locked the doors then rested his head on the steering wheel for a few minutes. He couldn't recall ever being so struck by one man before. How could less than ten minutes in one person's presence have affected him so dramatically? His dick ached. His hands shook. A small part of him wanted to head straight back to the cabin, the rest was far too scared.

"Idiot." A man like Evrain Brookes was hardly going to take the slightest bit of notice of his grandmother's gardener.

Dominic got his key into the ignition on the third attempt. He did a ropey three-point turn, narrowly avoiding the compact car parked behind him, which he guessed had to be Evrain's. It was fortunate that he'd driven the same route many times before because when he reached home he couldn't recall the journey at all. He parked in front of the diner in his usual spot, locked the truck then walked around the side of the building to the fire-escape steps. He had his own private entrance to the apartment on the first floor of the building. There was another staircase through the back of the diner but he didn't feel like making small talk with the regulars, or with Annie, the owner and his landlord.

Dominic's apartment was more spacious than it appeared from the outside. It stretched the full length of the upper floor of the building and had originally been designed as a vacation let for tourists. Annie had done a lovely job of making the place homey with some small touches of luxury. The rugs, pictures and knick-knacks in the lounge-diner were all purchased from local craftspeople. The kitchen was modern and sleek while the single large bedroom had been decorated to attract young couples. There was even a four-poster bed that had come from a grand house sale somewhere in Colorado.

Annie had gotten fed up of the constant round of cleaning and laundry that a rental property required. It was too much alongside her busy workload running the diner and she had decided that a longer term let would suit her better. Dominic was a regular customer and she'd overheard him talking about how his lease was running out. She'd offered the apartment to him on the spot and traded part of the rent for gardening services. He provided and maintained all the hanging baskets and pots that decorated the front of the diner, which proved to be great promotion for both his business and Annie's. It was a great deal all round, and Dominic took care of the place well. It was his sanctuary.

He crossed the threshold, then pulled the door firmly closed behind him. The sense of calm that usually enveloped him inside his home was absent. He sighed, bending to unlace his work boots. He pulled them off and put them on the piece of newspaper laid next to the front door. He'd get round to cleaning them later, but for now, he needed a shower.

Dominic emptied his pockets onto the kitchen counter. Keys, a few dollars in change, a small wad of tissue with some seeds snugly wrapped inside it and a clean handkerchief made a small pile. He padded into his bedroom, pausing to turn on a lamp that stood on his chest of drawers. He lowered the blinds, shutting out the darkness. Rolling his shoulders, he scanned the room. Something seemed off, but he couldn't work out what it was. Everything was in the same place he'd left it early that morning. Feeling utterly childish, he bent to look under the bed. Apart from a few scary dust bunnies there was nothing there.

"Jesus, Dom. Next you'll be checking the closet for the bogeyman." He laughed at his own nerves, trying to shake off the prickling sensation that had gooseflesh popping up on his arms. He pulled off his clothes, throwing the whole lot into the hamper just inside the door of his en-suite bathroom. He felt so hot—it was a relief to be naked in the cool room. Feeling a little giddy, he retreated to the bed, sat on the edge of the mattress and grimaced at the intense heat that enveloped his groin and painful erection.

"Absinthe, adder's tongue, agrimony, allspice, aloe..." he recited a long list of herbs. "Fennel, fenugreek, feverfew..." Dominic groaned. It wasn't working. Normally, reciting alphabetical lists took his mind away from his body and softened his errant dick. In the privacy of his home, he could have taken advantage of his hand and jacked off some frustration, but he just didn't fancy it. He shook his head. *Since when is a bit of manual relief not an attractive option?* He was already at 'f'—usually he got to dock and boredom set in, but not today. Evrain Brookes haunted his thoughts.

Dominic took a shower, the water as cold as he could bear it, needles stinging his skin. He sluiced away soap and shampoo and rested his forehead against the tiles. His rebellious body still resisted all attempts to cool its ardor. He rubbed himself down roughly with a towel then stalked naked into the bedroom, annoyed at his own lack of control. He lay down on the narrow bed and wrapped his hand around his cock with little enthusiasm. The velvety sheath slid easily beneath his hand he was so slick with pre-cum, but he forced himself to move slowly. His eyes closed and his thoughts drifted.

The lightest of touches tickled Dominic's bare shoulder. He twitched, shrugging it away, and carried on tormenting himself with featherlight strokes to his hypersensitive shaft. A minute or two later, the sensation returned, so light Dominic wasn't sure if it was real or his imagination. He continued to pet himself gently but opened his eyes to identify the source of irritation—probably a stray feather sticking out of his pillow. He blinked. He was seeing things. A slender green tendril curled over his upper arm—it seemed to be growing out of the wooden headboard. Leaves sprouted from the shoot and he recognized the distinctive shape as oak.

"Dreaming. I must be dreaming," Dominic muttered. As dreams went it was one of the most vivid he'd ever experienced. The delicate pressure on his skin was all too real. Erection forgotten, Dominic prodded at the stem. It was cool to his touch but there was the slightest vibration, almost as if the plant were breathing. As he watched, the stem circled his upper arm once, then again. He flexed his biceps as it squeezed a little, digging into his flesh.

He flinched as something slithered across his ankle. A second stem, issuing from one of the bottom corner posts of the bed was winding around his calf, pulling it so that his legs parted wider. Dominic bent his knee, tugging in an attempt to free himself but only managed to encourage the plant to hold him tighter. New shoots found his other limbs. Fresh, leafy growth embraced his wrists and ankles. Dominic found himself gradually pulled into a spread-eagle position on his bed. He yanked harder at the stems but they would not break.

They kept tugging until his naked body was stretched taut.

"Not a dream, this is a nightmare." But it seemed so real. The stems thickened, holding him in place as firmly as any chains could have. He was completely helpless.

Dominic attempted to slow his breathing and calm down. This was nothing more than a waking dream. Perhaps if he relaxed, his mind would allow him to awaken. One by one he allowed his muscles to release their tension, and for a few moments nothing happened. He was still held in place but his bonds stopped moving and growing. He gave himself a mental pat on the back. Dreams were nothing more than his subconscious playing tricks, or so he'd heard or read somewhere. His encounter with Evrain had stressed him out and now he was paying for it with some kind of erotic out-of-body experience. Except, as far as he was concerned, he was firmly inside his body and in control of his thoughts. For Christ's sake, he was tied to his own bed by a mutant oak! Tied down. Spread-eagled. Utterly exposed and defenseless. His cock, which had wilted a little, hardened into stiff rigidity.

Dominic moaned. His deepest, darkest fantasies were coming true. Secret longings that he had spoken about to no one, brought to the surface in a dream that had him doubting his sanity.

"No!" Dominic jerked his head up and strained to see what was going on farther down his body. A slim creeper wound sinuously around the base of his shaft, forming a living cock ring, ensuring that he stayed erect. The touch was torment. Strangely, Dominic wasn't scared. He still thrashed hard against the waxy green restraints in an attempt to free himself, but to no avail. The ache at his wrists and ankles just served to make him even harder. Pre-cum gleamed at his slit and his balls throbbed with heat. In his mind, he acknowledged that he would have been disappointed if his struggles had succeeded in breaking his bonds.

He stilled to gather his thoughts and calm his racing heart. *Accept the dream, Dom. Go with the flow. Admit you love this.* He closed his eyes and focused on the grip of the plant. He would probably have bruises by the morning where he'd fought, but now there was no attempt to squeeze or hurt him. His hands and feet were not tingling or cold so his circulation wasn't affected. That gave him comfort. The stems had made no attempt to encircle his neck or cause him harm. The message was clear. If he submitted, he had nothing to worry about.

Dominic felt the stirring of a breeze around his body. He hadn't opened a window because the night air had an intense chill. There had to be a draft coming from somewhere that he hadn't noticed before. This seemed more directed, though. It was as if someone was gently blowing warm, moist air across the head of his cock. He craned his neck to look but there was nothing to see. He was giving himself neck ache and let his head collapse back against the pillows. The soft sensation was maddening. It didn't provide nearly enough stimulation for him to come, instead it had him craving more. A proper touch.

From the corner of his eye he caught movement. Jerking his head from side to side, he watched as new shoots appeared from the bedposts. Not stiff enough to be termed twigs, they were more like vines or creeping ivy, but covered with oak leaves. The plant seemed sentient, moving with purpose. Assaulting from both sides, tiny tendrils tightened around his nipples, squeezing to the point of pain. Dominic gasped and arched his back only to be pressed back to the bed by wider stems across his thighs. He threw his head back and yelled as fronds circled and squeezed his balls. Stimulation of so many sensitive spots at one time was unbearable. He was going to come. A part of him resisted the urge. He should not be gaining so much pleasure from this uninvited attack on his body.

Dominic sobbed desperately as new stems pushed their way back to tickle the edge of his hole. The thought that he might be penetrated crossed his mind and he clenched his ass cheeks defensively. The touches to his balls, his dick and his nipples continued. Little pinches and jabs that caused momentary, delicious pain.

"Oh God!" Dominic writhed and squirmed as much as he was able in his leafy restraints. There was no escape from the plant's attention. However much he wriggled, the stems were there, touching, probing. It was as if the thing was exploring, mapping every inch of his body. Testing every sensitive spot. Working out which areas gave Dominic most pleasure and most pain. He threw his head back, closed his eyes and gave in to the sensations coursing through him.

Sweat sheened his skin. Muscles clenched and relaxed. Limbs twitched as the plant found new spots to tickle. Held on the edge for what seemed like a lifetime, Dominic was desperate to come. His balls were drawn up tight, his dick leaking pre-cum that the plant seemed to delight in sliding through and spreading. He gradually became aware that most of his body had been left alone and all the various shoots were now concentrated on his groin. Stems curled the length of his shaft, probed at his hole, wrapped his balls in a tight grip. The strange cock ring loosened. Dominic screamed. He spasmed and orgasmed harder than he could ever remember having done before. Heat rushed through his body and his vision blanked. He didn't see stars, just layers of green. Emerald upon olive upon lime flashed before his eyes. He spurted again. Sticky secretions burst from the plant stems, leaving silvery trails on his skin. Dominic panted, his breath coming in short, sharp gasps. Then, as suddenly as they had appeared, the stems retreated — unwinding from his limbs, slithering across his skin and disappearing back into the wooden posts and headboard of his bed.

Freed from bondage, Dominic scrambled upright, close to hyperventilating in shock. If this was a dream, then he had serious issues. His limbs bore the indentations of the stems where they had been held down so tightly and the evidence of his own release was patently obvious. Across his thighs, his chest and abdomen, tacky, shiny paths marked where the plant had lain.

"What the hell?" Dominic pinched himself. He was wide awake. His face heated at the thought of how he had felt, how fear and ecstasy had combined in the heat of an incredible orgasm. He went to his knees and examined the bed. The wood was smooth and polished. It appeared no different from any other evening. Tentatively he let his fingertips brush across the pattern of the grain, circling small whorls, tracing the knots. Though warm, the furniture gave no indication that it had ever come alive or would again.

"Nuts. I am definitely going freaking nuts," Dominic muttered. He was a sweaty, sticky mess and desperately in need of another shower. Half expecting other inanimate objects in his room to come alive and molest him, he padded to the bathroom with a tumult of confused thoughts and disbelief falling through his mind.

This time, he used hot water. He scrubbed at his skin until all traces of sap — or whatever the hell it was that the plant had left on him — were gone.

"Why do I get the feeling that a plant just came on me?" He shuddered. Apart from reddened dents around his wrists and ankles, there was no other damage to his body. All the important parts were unharmed and intact. Dominic stayed in the shower until the water began to cool. He switched off the spray, sighing heavily, and grabbed a clean towel for a quick rubdown. He examined his reflection, softened by the misty moisture coating the bathroom mirror. Anxious eyes stared back at him. He massaged his temples, fighting off the beginnings of a headache. He had no idea how he was going to sleep, or ever be entirely at ease in his bed again.

Perhaps there was something in Aggie's tea that brought on hallucinations. Dominic tried to find a logical explanation for his experience. His mind needed a reason before it would settle. Sure, he was tired, but he usually was after a hard day's work and he'd never had weird dreams before. He could have touched a poisonous plant without realizing it — that was plausible, more so than Aggie giving him something unsafe. Unwilling to go back to bed naked, he pulled on a pair of thin, cotton sleep pants that rarely saw the light of day. He plumped up his pillows and grabbed a seed catalog that he'd been meaning to browse through, then took a breath and lay down. For a few minutes, he stared blindly at the catalog, convinced that his bed was going to start sprouting shoots any minute. When nothing happened he relaxed a little. The clock told him that it was only slightly after ten. Still early. Dominic resolved to read for a while, then he'd attempt to sleep. With the light on.

* * * *

Evrain lifted his fineliner pen from the paper and shoved it behind his ear. He took a step back from his table to get a better view of the piece he'd been working on. The surface was slightly tilted with a lip at the bottom edge holding his layouts in place. The double-page spread he regarded with a critical eye was from a graphic novel — a personal project rather than one of the book covers or advertising designs he earned his living from. He smiled, satisfied that he had achieved exactly the expression he wanted. Dominic Castine's pretty face now adorned his central character. He was the perfect muse for debauched innocence, his eyes yaoi-huge, glistening with unshed tears.

Evrain wished the scenes he had been drawing could be real. Dark green leaves and curling stems against that creamy skin would look delicious. He could almost feel Dominic's indignation at being tied down and ravished against his will.

"I think you'd secretly enjoy it, Dominic," Evrain whispered to himself. "You'd fight but you would submit eventually and take pleasure from every illicit touch." He cast a critical eye across his work. Just because it was for his eyes only didn't mean that he lost any of his perfectionist streak. He knew the work was good. It came easily to him, even more so since he'd come into his powers. If he used natural inks, he could move the fluid on the page with a thought. It was one of the few things he could manage with any degree of control, probably because when he worked he could blank out all distractions and focus absolutely. Gregory assured him that natural talent underpinned what he did, it was just enhanced by his gift.

It had been one of their more normal telephone conversations.

"Evrain, you'll learn that there are ways to use your power to your advantage without frightening the natives. Warlocks do not exist outside fiction to 99.999 percent recurring of the population. Please try to remember that."

"I'm hardly going to forget, Gregory. I don't want to be consigned to Arkham along with the rest of the fictional psychopaths for the rest of my life, but there has to be some advantage to being a freak of nature."

Gregory had sighed. "You — we — are not freaks. We are…anomalies. A slight aberration in the evolutionary process and of course there are advantages, you are just not proficient enough to realize them yet."

"So how do you benefit from what you can do, Gregory?" It had been something they hadn't discussed.

"I have interests in several companies and own a great deal of real estate, but that's not how I made my money," Gregory had said. "After I graduated I went into the oil exploration business. I'm closest to water and earth elements. I can feel the earth, sense changes in density below ground. Once I'd felt one oil deposit, I could recognize another and another. I gained a reputation as an expert in oil discovery and that's a very lucrative career when you keep getting it right. It can also be explained by science, technology and, to a certain extent, luck."

"Hmm. I don't really fancy being the next J.R. Ewing, or moving to Texas. Too bloody hot."

"You've yet to work out where your strongest elemental affinities lie, Evrain. When you do, then you can worry about how to use your powers to your advantage. Without harming others, mind you. We can be selfish to some extent but not deliberately to the detriment of others, that's a big no-no."

"So there is a dark side to all this then?"

"Evrain, you are not too old to get a spanking, and believe me, if you start quoting *Star Wars* at me I will be on the next flight up there just to deliver one."

There had been a pause while Evrain had taken that in. Spanking was something he often fantasized about delivering. He had no desire to be the recipient.

"You're rolling your eyes, aren't you?" Gregory had added. "Stop it."

"Do you have cameras hidden in my apartment, Gregory? Never mind. I don't want to know."

Evrain had ended the conversation quickly after that. He was still no closer to understanding which elements might become his favorites—he was equally drawn to all four. In the meantime, if he could improve his artwork even a little, he'd take it. He checked his watch. It was almost half past ten, so too late to drive back to Hood River in order to deliver his grandmother's pot of balm to the delicious Dominic Castine. He would save that treat for the morning. The next day was Saturday. He wasn't sure if Dominic worked weekends but he'd take a chance and call in before going for a hike. Of course, if Dominic invited him in, he wouldn't turn down an alternative form of exercise.

Chapter Six

Evrain parked opposite the diner in Hood River. He'd found the prospect of seeing Dominic again more attractive than a Saturday morning lie-in. Waking early, he'd had a quick shower and shave, dressed for hiking then jumped in the car. He'd not bothered to eat, deciding that trying out the diner Dominic lived over could be a good way of persuading the shy young man to spend some time with him. Now he sat in his vehicle, quelling nervousness that he was unaccustomed to dealing with. He gripped Agatha's little jar of balm, tapping the lid with a forefinger.

"Jesus, get a grip, Evrain. He's a man, not a three-headed alien from Pluto." *A man I desperately want to get my hands on and cock into.* His thoughts were honest at least. It wasn't just the physical attraction, though—he felt drawn to Dominic. After such a brief meeting, it was odd that he couldn't get the man out of his head. He'd suspect that his grandmother had doped him with a love potion if he didn't know better.

He got out of the car and shut the door with a decisive slam. Just as he was about to cross the road, a figure descended the fire escape at the side of the building. The dark red hair was confirmation enough that it was Dominic even before Evrain saw his face. He grinned and leaned against the car, waiting for Dominic to spot him.

Evrain knew the exact moment that Dominic realized he was there. He froze. His lips parted. He glanced around as if checking out escape routes. *Oh, no, you don't.* Evrain crossed the road before Dominic had the chance to make a run for it. He didn't look either way, just marched across the road with his sights firmly fixed on Dominic. It was a good job there wasn't any traffic because Evrain's sense of self-preservation had completely deserted him. Dominic didn't move other than to hunch his shoulders slightly. Tension was apparent in every inch of his lean frame.

Evrain got right into Dominic's personal space. Dominic backed up until his ass hit the diner window.

"Good morning," Evrain said. He leaned in and pressed his lips to Dominic's. It was a very chaste kiss but Dominic still blushed to the roots of his hair.

"Wh-wha, what are you doing…here? Here. What are you doing *here*?" Dominic fumbled over his words. He ran his tongue over his lower lip as if gathering Evrain's taste.

"I'm here to take you to breakfast." Evrain only made that decision as the words left his mouth.

"I don't understand." Dominic's gaze darted around. His fingers clenched and unclenched.

"Breakfast. The first meal of the day. Generally involves bacon for anyone living on this continent."

Evrain paused. "I apologize. I've just stereotyped an entire nation or two."

"Three if you include Mexico," Dominic muttered.

Evrain grinned. There was a spark beneath the shyness. "So, are you hungry?"

"I don't... I mean, you can't just..."

Oh God, he's adorable. "It's breakfast, Dominic, and I'm buying. Indulge me."

"But why?" Dominic shuffled his feet and examined the ground.

"Why not?" Evrain put a finger beneath Dominic's chin and tilted it up. "That's better. You have such pretty eyes." He pushed his knee forwards, parting Dominic's legs. "You're getting hard for me, aren't you?"

"No!" Dominic twisted sideways in an attempt to get around Evrain. Evrain let him go. Dominic took a few steps then stopped. "What do you want, Evrain?"

"Breakfast. I have a thing for pancakes." He strolled toward the diner door, praying that Dominic would follow. He checked over his shoulder when he was halfway through the door.

Dominic's expression was a perfect mix of confused irritation and arousal. Evrain recognized the moment that Dominic gave in. His shoulders dropped and he sighed with a slight shake of his head. Evrain didn't hide his grin. He held the door open and waited until Dominic joined him.

"Coffee, boys?" The woman staffing the counter raised the jug and waggled it. "Morning, Dominic." Her eyebrow lifted, her curiosity evident.

"Yes, please," Evrain said. He scanned the available tables and took one near the back, next to the window. "It's warm in here." He peeled off the fleece he'd worn over his hiking skins. The light top beneath clung to his body and he wanted to see Dominic's reaction.

Dominic's eyes widened. He groaned and threw himself into a chair, shunting it under the table to hide his lap. He picked up a menu and hid behind it. Evrain pulled the laminated card away and placed it on the table.

"No hiding."

Dominic shivered.

Interesting, he's so responsive to commands. Definitely submissive, even if he doesn't know it. He'll fight and I'll enjoy the battle.

The waitress arrived with two mugs of coffee. "You guys know what you want?" she asked, placing a mug before each of them.

"The usual please, Annie." There was the tiniest quiver in Dominic's voice.

"I'll have what he's having," Evrain said. "Providing it includes pancakes. And bacon."

"Oh, it does. Pancakes, bacon, hash browns, grilled tomatoes. Wholewheat toast on the side. Warm syrup. Our Dom has a healthy appetite." Annie winked, full of mischief.

"As do I." Evrain winked right back.

She grinned, then laughed, the sound joyful. "Oh, it's about time!" She wandered off, hips swaying. "Shout if you need refills, food will be out in a few."

Evrain leaned back in his chair. He stretched his legs, ensuring that his calf brushed against Dominic's. He pulled Agatha's jar of balm from his pocket.

"I brought this for you." He placed the jar on the table and pushed it toward Dominic. "Grandma told me you hurt your back."

"It's nothing. Sore muscles, that's all." Dominic made eye contact. "But thank you for bringing it. You needn't have come all this way."

"It was just an excuse to see you again." Evrain shrugged. "I was tempted to drive back last night, but I was...working." He recalled his artwork and immediately pictured Dominic, naked and bound. Evrain's cock jerked. He shifted in his seat. "You shot out of Grandma's place so fast yesterday evening and I wanted a chance to get to know you better."

"Because I work for Aggie and you want to check me out?"

"No." Evrain chuckled. "Because I have evil intent when it comes to your hot body."

Dominic's mouth dropped open. "You're deliberately trying to shock me, aren't you?"

Their food arrived. Evrain tucked in and devoured several mouthfuls before he answered. "Not at all. Just giving you fair warning. God, this food is amazing. I can see this becoming a regular haunt of mine."

Dominic stared at him for a few seconds as if he couldn't quite believe what he was hearing. He gave an exasperated sigh and began to eat. Evrain kept half an eye on Dominic while they finished their meal and found himself entranced. Dominic ate efficiently, that was the only way Evrain could think to describe the neat sectioning of food, the precise cutting. The slide of the fork between Dominic's lips made Evrain wish that it could be his cock there instead.

Dominic finally pushed his plate aside. "So what now?"

"That's up to you." Evrain swallowed the last of his coffee. "Would you like me to leave?"

"I…" Dominic tore his napkin into tiny shreds, making a neat pile of the pieces on the table. He clearly hadn't expected to be given that option. "No. I mean, that is, if you want…"

"Oh, I do want. Will you let me seduce you, Dominic? There's something between us that I'd like to explore and I know you feel it too."

"Seduce me?" Dominic's voice rose. "How am I supposed to answer that?"

"By calming down, sweetheart. I'm not going to jump you in public — that kind of exhibitionism does nothing for me. Do you have to work this morning?"

Dominic nodded. "I'm clearing the pots and baskets here, then replanting."

"Well, I'll help. I was going to go for a hike, but I'd much rather spend time with you."

"Do you know anything about gardening?" Dominic asked.

"Let's just say I have an affinity for the earth and all things green."

"I don't know if that's a yes or a no."

"I can follow instructions."

"Really? From what I've seen so far, I assumed you preferred to give the orders?" Dominic's skepticism was almost comical.

"That's true in most situations, especially in the bedroom." Evrain paused for dramatic effect. "But in the garden I will submit…to your expertise." Evrain emphasized the word 'submit', observing Dominic's expression carefully. The hint of pink highlighting his cheekbones deepened.

Evrain left some bills on the table and stood up. "Shall we go then? I can't wait for you to start bossing me around."

"I can pay for my own breakfast." Dominic stood but made no move to leave.

"I believe I invited you, so it's my treat. I think our first date is going well, don't you?"

That got Dominic moving. Evrain followed him outside, pulling on his fleece as he walked.

"I don't know what this is, but it isn't a date," Dominic muttered under his breath. "More like a hostile takeover."

* * * *

Evrain discovered that he enjoyed planting. Probing the warm compost with a finger to make a hole, dropping the plants in then bedding them down was satisfying work. Dominic had a portable radio that he balanced on the wall next to them. The local station played a mixture of pop and rock, interspersed with entertaining, if cheesy, commercials for local businesses. The music gave a beat to the rhythm of the work and Evrain hummed along. Every now and again, he caught Dominic giving him a sideways glance. It was a shame it wasn't warmer, then he could have stripped off his shirt and given Dominic something to really look at. They could form a mutual appreciation society—Evrain was certain that Dominic must be nicely ripped. He licked his lips.

"Are you thirsty?" Dominic asked. "Annie will give us bottled water if you want some."

"I'm good. Maybe later."

They carried on working in silence for a while until Dominic paused.

"I need to fetch the trays of seedlings for the hanging baskets."

"Need a hand?" Evrain asked, rising from where he'd been kneeling on the floor finishing off a pot.

Dominic shrugged so Evrain took that as an invitation. He followed Dominic around to the back of the building where there was a small parking lot. In one corner, there was a storage shack. It didn't merit the title of shed in Evrain's opinion. It seemed to be constructed from a converted freight box of some kind.

"I keep some equipment here for my business. The trays of plants are inside." Dominic pulled open the heavy door.

Inside it was very dark. Evrain could just make out the shape of a mower, some kind of spray pump and a few sacks of compost. Tools hung in neat rows on the walls. Dominic disappeared into the darkness. Evrain glanced across the lot—there was nobody around. He followed Dominic and pulled the door closed behind him, enclosing them both in the warm, dark space.

Evrain focused his senses. Scents surrounded him, earthy and sweet. He could hear Dominic's breathing, faster than it should be.

"What..."

Before Dominic could get another word out, Evrain gathered him into a firm embrace. "I've been wanting to do this all morning." He pressed his lips to Dominic's, probing the seam with his tongue. Evrain was even more assertive than first thing that morning when he'd tasted Dominic for the first time. His lips were so soft. *Let me in, darling.*

Dominic stood stiff in Evrain's hold. Evrain slipped an arm around his hips then cupped Dominic's ass. Dominic gasped, his lips parted, and Evrain took full advantage, thrusting his tongue into Dominic's mouth. He pulled Dominic closer until they were pressed together, groin to groin. Dominic's erection stabbed at him through the layers of their clothing. He ravished Dominic's mouth, keeping him distracted while he slipped his hand down the back of Dominic's cargo pants. His ass was firm, well muscled and warm. Evrain squeezed a cheek then probed Dominic's crack with his finger. Dominic squirmed and moaned. He pulled away from the kiss.

"Stop! Stop, Evrain."

"Why?" Evrain stilled. "I think we're both enjoying this."

"I'll… I'll come!"

"Oh, is that all? That's the general idea." Evrain pushed the dry tip of his finger past Dominic's fluttering guardian muscle.

Dominic fumbled with his zipper. He yanked his pants and underwear down to midthigh, then grasped his rigid cock.

"That's mine." Evrain slapped Dominic's hand away, replacing it with his own. "So hot." Two swift tugs and Dominic came in a hot gush over Evrain's hand.

"Oh God!" Dominic panted. "This isn't right."

"Feels right to me." Evrain chuckled, pulling Dominic closer again.

"You're, you're… Do you want…? Oh God." Dominic rested his head on Evrain's shoulder. Heat poured from his body.

"You don't have to do anything, Dominic." Evrain gave himself a few points for self-control. "That was for you."

Dominic sank to his knees. He unfastened Evrain's pants, letting his cock spring free. Evrain locked his knees, parted his legs a little farther. He wished there was more light. What he wouldn't give to watch Dominic's pretty mouth taking him in.

Wet heat surrounded Evrain's dick as Dominic began to suck. He went at his task with enthusiasm, keeping his teeth covered apart from the occasional light scrape. Evrain sucked in his breath. Dominic had a talented mouth. He was going to get Evrain off in seconds.

Evrain grabbed a handful of Dominic's hair, holding him in place. He waited to see if Dominic fought against the hold, but he didn't. There was no resistance. Evrain jerked his hips, fucking Dominic's willing mouth. Dominic submitted totally, allowing Evrain control. On the edge of orgasm, Evrain loosened his grip on Dominic's hair, giving him a chance to pull away.

"Close." The word came out as a hiss. Dominic sucked harder, taking Evrain's shaft deep into his throat. Evrain came hard, muscles trembling. Dominic swallowed every drop, then licked Evrain's shaft clean before letting it slip from his lips. For a few moments, the only sound was their heavy breathing.

Dominic was the first to move. He pushed open the door, flooding the storage container with light. Evrain blinked as the brightness temporarily blinded him. He spotted a rag and cleaned off his hands before yanking up his pants. Dominic quickly adjusted his clothing too. He picked up a couple of trays of plants and without a word headed back toward the diner.

Smug didn't begin to describe how Evrain felt. He hefted a couple of trays of seedlings and set off after Dominic. Fabric rubbed his oversensitized cock with every step. At the front of the diner there was no sign of Dominic. Evrain perched on the wall and waited. He didn't want to carry on working and get things wrong.

After a couple of minutes, Dominic appeared from inside the diner, clutching a couple of bottles of Gatorade. He thrust one into Evrain's hand without a word. He didn't make eye contact and his cheeks were glowing scarlet. Evrain took the drink. He didn't need to push. He had Dominic well and truly in his clutches. There was nowhere for Dominic to run or hide. Evrain was content to take his time. Other opportunities like today would present themselves. The thrill of the hunt coursed through his veins. Sooner or later, Dominic would realize that resistance was futile. Evrain knew, deep down, that they were meant to be together.

Is this what love at first sight feels like? He watched Dominic's Adam's apple bob and he chugged down his drink. *Every bit of him turns me on, yet I don't know him, not really.* Dominic wiped his mouth with the back of his hand—his lips were puffy, kiss-swollen. He gave Evrain a shy smile. Not wanting to spoil the moment, Evrain just smiled back.

Chapter Seven

Agatha poured herself a small sherry in celebration. She gave the glass of amber liquid a critical glance and added a bit more. *Better.* Her plans for Evrain were beginning to come together and that was worthy of a drink or two. Since she had engineered a meeting between Evrain and Dominic, the two young men had become a little closer. Of course, that was inevitable. She had never seen two auras more compatible. The only couple she knew that came near were Gregory and Coryn. She suspected that Evrain would like to move faster, much faster, but for once he was managing to temper his impatience and give Dominic the time and space he needed. Agatha had no doubt that Dominic was interested. Whenever he and Evrain crossed paths, the air crackled with the sparks of attraction.

She had watched with interest and pleasure as Dominic had progressed from complete avoidance to tentative conversation and shy smiles. It was fascinating. Something had triggered the change. Aggie suspected it had something to do with her pot of balm and the manner of its delivery, but when she had questioned Evrain about it he'd clammed up and just given her an enigmatic smile. *More mysterious than the Mona Lisa, damn it. I want details!*

A side effect of the burgeoning relationship between Evrain and Dominic was that Evrain visited Hornbeam Cottage more and more. Agatha was under no illusions about the reason for his visits. It certainly wasn't to see her and subject himself to more loving abuse as she attempted to imbue in him the discipline he needed to control his powers. If Dominic was around, even out in the garden, Evrain's lessons went well. If he was absent, Agatha kept a fire extinguisher to hand. She wished that Gregory could visit more. Evrain really needed the guidance of another elemental warlock. She did her best but she was a poor substitute for someone who lived and breathed the power as Gregory did, but Gregory had his own life to lead and it was at the other end of the country.

The evening air was chilly and damp. Agatha tossed another log on the fire and settled in her favorite armchair with a book, her tipple on a side table within easy reach. She pulled a blanket fashioned from squares of multicolored wool across her lap. It wasn't one of the evenings for the shows she was addicted to, so the television remained off. She had no need of constant background chatter. She'd just opened the thriller she was reading to her marked page when the phone rang. She gave a heavy sigh, grumbling as she picked up the receiver.

"Yes, who is it?"

"Aggie, it's Gregory."

"Good grief. Were your ears burning? I was just thinking about you."

"All good thoughts, I hope," Gregory said. He sounded more subdued than usual.

"Not all." She chuckled. "When are you heading northward next? Evrain needs you."

"I talk to him almost every day, Aggie, give me a break. The boy does not need me hanging round his neck. He has to feel his own way, make a few mistakes. Blister his fingertips a few times. It's all part of the learning process."

"He's more likely to burn down half the state than singe an eyebrow, Gregory," Aggie snapped. "Or maybe flood downtown Portland. Did you know there have been reports on the news about waterspouts appearing on the river there? Was it wise to house him so close to the water?"

"Water spouts are a naturally occurring phenomenon. As are forest fires," Gregory said dryly. "If he creates a hurricane by mistake, or opens the San Andreas Fault line, give me a call." He paused. "That's not why I'm calling."

"That sounds ominous," Aggie said. "Is Coryn okay?"

"He's fine. He sends his love. Look, Aggie, I'll get to the point. Have you looked at your own aura recently?"

Aggie frowned. "No. I avoid that whenever possible, you know that. I keep an eye on Evrain's. He's in love so it's all glitter and pink sparkles at the moment."

"Love? With Dominic?"

"Of course. He might not realize it yet, but it's there. Plain as the nose on my face."

"That's fantastic news, you cunning old biddy. You should set up a matchmaking service."

Aggie preened even though Gregory couldn't see her. "I know, Dominic has such a calm center, he's perfect for Evrain. But what does my aura have to do with anything?"

"I don't want to worry you, but I've been hearing a few unpleasant rumors on the grapevine. Make sure your wards are up to date."

"That might warn me about magical interference, Gregory, but it won't do me any good if something more malevolent is heading my way. My charms are no defense against the kind of power Symeon could bring to bear if he chose. What have you heard?"

"A lot of gossip about Evrain. He's famous in certain circles—the covens in particular. I think Symeon Malus has been engaged in some kind of campaign. He's spreading rumors about how powerful, and how dangerous, Evrain is. He's creating enemies for Evrain, sowing the seeds of discord."

"Bah," Aggie scoffed. "Witches love a scandal. So long as Evrain doesn't start throwing his weight around, he'll soon become yesterday's news. I still don't get what this has to do with me."

Gregory sighed. "The easiest way to weaken an untrained warlock is to remove his safety nets. Those are you, me and now Dominic. I'm not in much danger. It will be a cold day in hell when Symeon gets the better of me."

"But I'm vulnerable. Dominic even more so." Aggie scrunched her brow into a frown. "I'll have to talk to Evrain about that. It's a shame, I would have liked to keep him shielded from this kind of thing a while longer yet."

"Which I imagine Symeon will guess and want to use to his advantage. He'll try to get Evrain into a position where teaming up will seem like a favorable option. To do that he needs to get people out of the way who will advise him otherwise. It wouldn't surprise me if Symeon has already been in touch. Has Evrain said anything?"

"No, he hasn't." Agatha stared into the flames. "There's no messing with fate, Gregory. If my time is here, then there's little I can do about it."

"Just be careful, okay? Lock your damn door for once, old woman."

"I'll give you old... You watch yourself too, Gregory. Keep Coryn close."

"Always." Gregory rang off.

Aggie put her book aside, unable to concentrate. The words just ran together on the page. She stood, pulled the blanket around her shoulders. She collected a letter opener – solid silver, it might provide a useful form of defense – then went outside. It was a clear night – no moon, but plenty of stars sparkled like glitter across a dark velvet cloth. A light breeze rustled the surrounding trees. Agatha raised her hand and focused on it, searching for the colors of her aura. They had faded over time, shades of green muted rather than vibrant. The colors were comfortable, familiar. When she was sick, there were threads of gray. Love had woven warm rose and fuchsia through the green. Now she saw only darkness. Black with streaks of blood red.

"Soon then." She sighed and gazed at the night sky. "Sooner than I would have liked." A wave of dizziness passed over her. She leaned on the garden gate letting the sensation pass. A twig snapped. Agatha realized she wasn't alone. She stood listening to the sounds of the night, familiar but not quite right. A chill crept up her spine. She froze in place, scanning her surroundings, seeking any sign of another presence. If someone were there, he or she was probably watching. Waiting. She took a few steps back toward the cabin then stopped to listen again. Her heart pounded.

Get inside, stupid old woman. She backed toward the door, taking small, silent steps. In the distance a shadow separated from the trees, the rough outline of a figure revealing itself. The figure approached steadily. Agatha realized that the light from the open door behind her would show her shape just as surely as if it had been broad daylight. She pulled the door closed, choosing to meet her assailant in the open air. There was no point in running. No time to get to the phone and call for help—little good that it would do. The cabin was too remote for assistance to arrive with any speed. Certainly not fast enough to help her now.

She tightened her fingers around the handle of the letter opener. It wouldn't save her, but if she could draw blood, leave a clue for investigators to follow, then she would. She gripped her weapon in both hands and dropped to a slight crouch. There was nowhere left to go, nothing to do but wait.

The dark figure reached the gate, growing larger. It didn't open the gate or vault it—the thing came *through* the gate. Agatha could see now that it was formed from mud or clay. Not a man but a monster. This had to be Symeon Malus' work. In the seconds she had left, she realized that Symeon could not be working alone. This evil sorcery was not the work of one man—she could smell the witchcraft animating the creature. It came at her at a lumbering run. She held up the silver knife, knowing that it would be useless.

Then it was on top of her, overwhelming her, a suffocating avalanche of mud blocking her nose, her eyes, her mouth. The thing's momentum knocked Agatha from her feet. She slashed her weapon from side to side but it slid through the muck her attacker was created from with little resistance. She tried to cry out, but her breath was gone. All her senses failed under the onslaught. Agatha prayed for it to be over. False light flashed before her eyes. The final vestiges of panic and pain were swept away by silence.

* * * *

Evrain checked that he'd locked his car and set off down the path to Agatha's cabin, carrying the sack of groceries he'd picked up for her. It was a bright day and the comfortable warmth spoke of early summer sunshine to come. He had a morning of training ahead of him but he'd arranged to meet Dominic for lunch and that had him whistling as he walked. He planned to extend lunch to an afternoon date, one that would preferably turn into an overnight stay. *It's about time!* Since their delicious encounter in Dominic's tool store, they had been edging around each other. Evrain stole kisses when he could, spent as much time with Dominic as he could and Dominic showed every sign that he was up for more, but when it came to the crunch, Dominic's shyness always got in the way. Evrain was running out of patience. He needed to claim his man, something that was long overdue.

He pushed open Agatha's gate and pulled his hand away.

"Ugh! What the hell...?" His fingers were covered in mud. On closer inspection, he could see that the top bar of the gate was covered in mucky residue. He rubbed his hands together, brushing off as much dirt as he could. The path to the cottage was also muddy. "What have you been up to, Grandma?" Evrain murmured. He approached the door, which stood open just a crack. He checked around in case his grandmother was outside pottering but there was no sign of her so he pushed open the door. Inside the cabin everything was still and silent. It was quiet. Far too quiet.

Evrain paused in the doorway, taking everything in. Usually the kettle would be bubbling away, there would be the aroma of fresh baking, curtains fluttering in the breeze from open windows. Today there was nothing. He took a couple of steps inside and caught sight of Agatha's hand resting on the arm of her favorite chair, the top of her head just visible. The chair's back was to Evrain so he couldn't see more. He put the bag of groceries on the kitchen counter and unpacked a few of the tins and jars. His grandmother didn't stir.

"Are you dozing, Grandma?" Evrain spoke quietly — he didn't want to disturb Agatha if she was snoozing. He walked toward the fire, which was cold, just ashes in the grate. Evrain gasped in horror. Agatha sat in her chair but her head lolled forward. What he could see of her face was mottled blue and swollen, her puffy tongue poking from between her lips. There was no question that she was dead and, from the expression of utter horror on her face, her passing had not been easy.

Evrain's stomach rolled. He dashed outside and retched, vomiting until his guts were empty. He sobbed, tears rolling down his face. Frantically he grabbed his phone from his back pocket and dialed nine-one-one.

Waiting for the cops to arrive was the longest twenty minutes of Evrain's life. He sat on the edge of the garden path with his head between his knees for part of it, then got up and paced up and down. He'd managed to give detailed directions and soon Hornbeam Cottage was swarming with cops, paramedics and, not long after, crime scene techs. Evrain found himself walking down the lane with a detective, answering questions as best he could. He ended up sat in the front seat of a black and white, sipping a cup of coffee. It helped steady his nerves because his new detective friend had slipped a dose of brandy from his hipflask into Evrain's cardboard cup.

"You're in shock. Sit here quietly and tell me what you remember. It's important I get your first impressions down before you forget."

"Detective O'Shea, I'd need bleach and a scouring pad to get that image out of my mind. I'm not likely to forget in a hurry."

The detective pulled out a notepad and pen. "In your own time, son."

Evrain recited the details of his morning. There wasn't much to tell. He described finding the cabin door ajar, the silence and the shocking realization that Agatha was dead.

"I didn't see anyone from the time I parked the car to the time I left the cottage to call you. Not a soul," Evrain said.

"And you didn't notice anything unusual or out of place? The tiniest thing could help." O'Shea waited, pen poised.

"No." Evrain paused. "There was something. The gate... It had mud on the top. How would it have got there?"

"I'll let the crime scene guys know to get it tested. Now, apart from yourself, did your grandma have any regular visitors?"

"She was sociable. She had lots of people from the town dropping in for her herbal remedies. Oh... Dominic! I need to call him." Evrain had no idea how he would break the news.

"Dominic?" O'Shea asked.

"Sorry. Dominic Castine. He takes care of the garden and is at my grandmother's most weekends and a couple of evenings a week. I suppose you should know... He and I are...close."

O'Shea didn't blink. Evrain was impressed.

"Thanks for your openness, Mr. Brookes. Now, I have to ask this. Where were you last night and can anyone confirm your whereabouts?"

"I worked until seven—I work at ThInk in Portland—then went straight on to a client dinner at the Marriott in the evening. My boss was there—I can give you his details. It wound up around midnight and I went home."

"You live in Portland?"

"Yes. The security cameras on my building's parking garage should confirm when I got back and when I left again this morning to drive over here. Between a quarter past midnight and seven I was alone. I stopped for a drive-through breakfast—the receipt is probably still in the car. The breakfast is all over the path at the cabin, where I threw up." Evrain gave the detective his address details, a contact number for his boss and Dominic's cell number.

"I'm sorry for your loss," O'Shea said, sounding genuinely sympathetic. "If you think of anything else" — he handed over a card — "call me any time. I'll let you know when you can go back into the house."

"She wasn't ill, you know," Evrain said. "Grandma was in great health for her age."

"Well, from what I saw, son, and I'm not a medical expert, that didn't seem like a death from natural causes. I won't speculate but did she have any enemies?"

"Not that I know of, but local people might have more of a clue than I do. I only moved out here from Scotland a few months ago."

"Okay. I'll need you to come down to the precinct and make a statement."

"I can do that whenever suits," Evrain said. "I want this bastard caught." Anger started to take over from shock and bewilderment.

"Go home, Mr. Brookes. Is there anyone you can call to be with you?"

"Yes, I'll be fine. Really."

Evrain left the security of the cop car and got behind the wheel of his own vehicle. He drove off with the intention of going home but found himself pulling up outside the diner. There was only one person he wanted to see. Dominic would come home to change before meeting Evrain for their date. He'd be able to head him off, protect him from the chaos at Agatha's and break the news gently. He couldn't do it over the phone and he had to tell Dominic before the police got in touch.

"Fuck it all to hell!" Evrain thumped the steering wheel. There was no way to lessen the impact of news he had barely absorbed himself, and the last thing in the world he wanted to do was hurt Dominic.

Chapter Eight

It was the kind of Dickensian office one might expect to see in the latest historical drama on the BBC and would definitely have felt more at home in Evrain's native Scotland than in Portland. A heavy dark-wood desk topped with green leather took center stage, the chair positioned behind it equally imposing. Shelves stuffed with leather-bound volumes, their spines glinting with dull-gold lettering, covered the walls. Evrain doubted that any of the musty tomes had been removed from their resting places in decades. The room smelled of wax polish and old paper. A cream blind covered the single window, muting the early morning light. Evrain was grateful for the lack of brightness. His head pounded with the persistent headache that had plagued him almost continually since his grandmother's death a month earlier. A month during which the police had failed to find a single clue as to who might have been Agatha's murderer. Not that their lack of progress surprised Evrain. Having discussed it frequently with Gregory, they were both convinced that Symeon Malus was behind Agatha's death. Gregory had related the conversation he'd had with Agatha on the night of her death. Evrain only wished she'd called him straight away. If he'd been there at the cabin, he might have put off her assailant and given them time to plan better protection. The wards at the cabin certainly hadn't helped her.

Evrain slumped in one of the matching leather chairs set before the desk. He wore a sober black suit and shirt but had not succumbed to his mother's telephoned pleading to find a tie. He'd worn one to the funeral, which had taken place a few days ago. That was enough of a concession to formality in Evrain's eyes.

Dominic balanced nervously on the edge of the other chair, looking like he might bolt from the room at any moment. He clasped his hands together in his lap so tightly that his knuckles were white.

"There's no need to be nervous, you know." Evrain felt a need to reassure Dominic, who jumped as if Evrain's voice had startled him.

"Sorry, it's just that I've never been summoned to a lawyer's office before. It's a little…intimidating." His glance darted everywhere, never settling in one place for long. "I should have dressed smarter."

"You are quite smart enough." *Stunning in fact. The blue of that shirt really brings out your eyes.* "My mother told me I should wear a tie, but it's Agatha's will we're hearing and she thought ties were modern-day nooses."

Dominic smiled, but the expression was forced.

"I can picture Dickens in here taking notes for scenes in *Bleak House*," Evrain said. "Mr. Vholes is likely to come creeping around the corner at any moment."

Dominic gave a nervous chuckle. "Dickens is a bit heavy for me, he takes far too long to get to the point."

"So who do you like to read?" Evrain seized the opportunity to learn a little more about Dominic, while helping him relax with mundane conversation.

"Nothing high-brow, I'm afraid. I like old-fashioned murder mysteries."

"Agatha Christie?"

"Yes, and I love the British TV series, you know — *Marple* and *Poirot*. But I like other writers as well — Dorothy L. Sayers, Margery Allingham. Oh, and I'm addicted to *Midsomer Murders*."

"Grandmother always told me she was named after Agatha Christie. Agatha was a friend of the family, apparently. Not sure I believe Grandma, she always had a ready supply of stories like that."

"There was so much I never got to know about her." Dominic sounded wistful. "I miss her. She was a great friend to me. She didn't deserve to die the way she did." His voice became fierce.

"No, she didn't." Evrain stood and paced. "And the more time that passes since her death, the less likely it is that the killer will be caught. The murderer could have been a ghost for all the trace he left."

"I'm sure the police are doing everything they can," Dominic said.

Evrain shrugged. "I suppose so. I just hate that her violent passing means she carries on being a victim. The autopsy, the delays before we could give her the funeral she wanted, and now this, finally settling her estate. It's dragged on, causing pain for everyone involved."

"You were close." It was a statement, not a question, and Evrain didn't feel obliged to answer. Dominic didn't know of the special bond between Evrain and his grandmother but he'd seen enough of them together to know they had a solid relationship.

"I always had more in common with her than I did with my parents. I was a bit rebellious as a teenager. My dad decided I'd be better off at boarding school where I couldn't be so much of a disruptive influence on my younger sisters. I spent most of my longer school holidays with Grandma or my godfather Gregory and his partner in Florida."

"I met Gregory once, briefly, when he was visiting Aggie," Dominic said. "She spoke about you all the time. I know she loved that you came to live over here." Dominic leaned forward, scrubbing a hand through his hair.

"Much good it did her." Evrain couldn't help the hint of bitterness that crept into his voice.

"What happened was not your fault," Dominic said with quiet certainty.

Evrain wished that he could be equally sure. He was saved from his doubts when the office door creaked open. Angus Pitt, the skeletal family solicitor, strolled into the room. He looked suitably somber, his entire demeanor cast in gray. Evrain shook hands with him, holding back a shiver at Pitt's cool, papery skin. Dominic stood and murmured a greeting, then they all sat down.

"Well, gentlemen, I would say it was nice to meet you, but the circumstances somewhat preclude that sentiment."

Evrain met the lawyer's shrewd gaze directly. "Indeed. My preference would be to get through matters as quickly as possible." He was craving fresh air.

Pitt blinked. "Just so." He produced a manila folder from his desk drawer, opened it then withdrew a slim sheaf of papers. "Very well, let us begin."

At least he didn't open with "Are we all sitting comfortably?" Evrain fought to keep still. Sarcasm hovered on the tip of his tongue.

"We are here to listen to the last will and testament of Agatha Millicent Hornbeam," Pitt continued, seemingly oblivious to Evrain's utter lack of respect.

"Um, excuse me, sir." Dominic held up his hand as if he were in a schoolroom.

Evrain growled. Dominic shouldn't be addressing anyone as 'sir' except him. He shook his head. *Where did that thought come from?*

"Yes, Mr. Castine?" Pitt peered over his glasses, apparently enjoying the deference.

"Should I leave?" Dominic asked. "This is family business, surely."

"Your presence is required. Please remain where you are."

"Oh. Okay." Dominic glanced across at Evrain, his expression anxious.

Evrain attempted a reassuring smile. It came as no surprise to him that Agatha had left something to Dominic in her will, though it was clear that Dominic had no idea.

Pitt mumbled through a quantity of legal jargon that Evrain paid little attention to. Dominic shuffled his feet, making a brave effort not to appear bored out of his mind. Evrain avoided fidgeting through strength of will alone. He tuned back into the man's droning voice.

"Other than some small bequests to beneficiaries who have been informed in writing, the two of you share the majority of the estate." Pitt then opened a small vellum packet that sat on the pile of papers on the desk in front of him. Two envelopes slid out. Pitt pushed them to the edge of the desk and gestured at them. "There is a letter here for each of you. Mrs. Hornbeam's instructions are that they must be opened on the day that you receive them, before the sun sets, and that you must be in each other's presence." Hooded eyes blinked slowly. "Her words, not mine."

Evrain stood. He picked up both envelopes and handed the one with Dominic's name inscribed on it to him. He examined his own. His name was written out in full in Agatha's spidery, copperplate hand. The paper was thick, creamy white. The ink blue-black. He turned the envelope over and found a blood-red wax seal, stamped with the shape of a flower.

As Evrain resumed his seat, Pitt picked up another document and began to read out the details of a series of small bequests, mainly to charities and old friends. Gregory and Coryn were both mentioned as were Evrain's sisters and his mother, who all inherited pieces of jewelry. For Evrain's father there was a particularly fine set of leather-bound encyclopedias that James had always admired.

Dominic fidgeted, clearly uncomfortable. Evrain assumed that he had no idea that Aggie had left him anything at all. It wasn't the kind of thing she would have talked about. Evrain's parents had told him that he, rather than they, would inherit Aggie's estate when the time came. He caught Dominic staring at him and returned the glance. Dominic's cheeks flushed deeply.

Caught you. Evrain hid his grin. A cough from in front of him brought his attention back to the proceedings.

"If I could have your attention, gentlemen?" Pitt scowled at them as if they were a couple of recalcitrant schoolboys. "Where was I...? Yes, to Dominic Castine I leave the land at Hornbeam Cottage, to include the gardens and surrounding acreage. In addition, a sum of one hundred thousand dollars to support the development of that land as part of his business."

Dominic gasped. "But that can't be right!"

"I can assure you, Mr. Castine, that it is correct." Pitt's nose wrinkled and his eyes narrowed, daring Dominic to dispute his words again. "And to my beloved grandson, Evrain James Brookes, Hornbeam Cottage and the remainder of the estate amounting to a value of some two million, five hundred thousand dollars, on condition that he makes Hornbeam Cottage his permanent residence with immediate effect."

Evrain drew in a sharp breath.

Pitt stood and gave a small bow. "I'll give you a few minutes' privacy while I organize some coffee. Needless to say, gentlemen, I would be honored to offer any further legal services you may require." He left the room quietly. The click of the closing door seemed to resound through the silence like a thunderclap.

"Holy fuck! I don't know about coffee, I feel the need for hard liquor." Evrain ran a hand through his hair. "I had no idea..."

Dominic stood but kept his head bowed, his pretty eyes firmly fixed on the Axminster. "I'm so sorry about this, Evrain. Please believe me when I say I knew nothing about the bequest, Aggie never said a word. I'll sign everything over to you. I'm sure Mr. Pitt can make the necessary arrangements and just deduct his fee or something. It should all be yours by rights, I don't know what Aggie was thinking. I never expected anything, she never said... I'm sorry this has happened. I'll sign whatever I need to sign and you won't have to see me again." He stumbled over the words then took a rough breath.

Evrain wondered if he'd need a paper bag. Dominic was on the verge of hyperventilating. He'd never heard so many words come out of the man's mouth in one go. He needed gagging before he got any more stupid. Now, there was an idea worth experimenting with. Evrain pictured Dominic's lips stretched around a ball gag and decided to add it to his list of things to do before he hit twenty-two. Most of the items on that list involved Dominic naked and a wide variety of restraints.

"Oh no, you don't." Evrain stood directly in front of Dominic. He put his hands on Dominic's shaking shoulders and squeezed lightly. "You don't escape me that easily." He kept his tone low and commanding. "My grandmother had good reasons for everything she did while she was alive and I have more sense than to question that now she's gone."

Dominic kept shaking his head. The words weren't sinking in.

Evrain squeezed a bit harder. "Look at me, Dominic."

No response. Coppery lashes still concealed Dominic's eyes.

"Look. At. Me."

Dominic jerked in Evrain's hold. He gasped as if shaken from a trance, then made eye contact. "Sorry. I'm just... I can't believe it!"

"Don't be sorry. You have nothing to apologize for." Evrain didn't loosen his grip. "I have no use for land. You do. I'm more than happy to let you commit yourself to hard labor in my stead."

"But all that money! I haven't earned it, any of it." Dominic sounded genuinely in distress.

"And you think I have?" Evrain cupped Dominic's face with one hand, expecting him to pull away. He didn't. "She's left me more than enough to ensure that I don't have to work again unless I want to. Cunning old biddy—I thought she was as poor as a church mouse, not rolling in loot."

Dominic trembled beneath his touch. It would only take a second to lean in and kiss the worry away. Evrain swayed toward Dominic. He had such lovely lips. Kissable. Or maybe a quick nip. Gentle pain to pull him out of his state of shock.

Dominic had lowered his eyes again. That wouldn't do. Evrain took a single step back and removed his hands from Dominic's body.

"Look at me."

Dominic shifted nervously but didn't meet his eyes.

"I said look at me, Dominic. Don't make me ask you again."

Anxious blue eyes gradually met his own. Evrain preened at another small victory. "Please believe that I'm happy for you." Evrain clasped his hands behind his back to stop from touching Dominic again. He had to move with glacial slowness or risk frightening his quarry away completely. "Accept that something good has come out of a horrific act. Aggie wanted this for you. For us. Accept it with grace."

Dominic gave a single nod. Evrain caught his breath as the light glinted in Dominic's hair, reflecting the warm, deep red tones. Evrain had a sudden urge to run his hands through it—he remembered how soft it felt. It was the perfect length to get a good grip, to tug Dominic's head back and hold him still for a punishing kiss. He lifted his hand, and Dominic froze. His body was sending out signals that said 'touch me, please touch me'. Whether his mind was thinking the same thing was debatable. Evrain didn't care. He felt the electric tension in the air, deciding that Dominic's lack of movement gave him permission to continue. However, his planned exploration was abruptly curtailed as the office door clicked open to admit Angus Pitt and his secretary, who was lugging a heavy tray of coffee.

Evrain scowled his annoyance and frustration but moved away. Dominic let out his breath with a slight shudder, making Evrain wonder if Dominic was about to laugh hysterically or sob with relief. He smiled. He liked having Dominic off balance. His vulnerability just made him all the more attractive to Evrain's predatory nature. That was tempered by a need to comfort and protect. He wanted nothing more than to pull Dominic into his arms and keep him safe.

Evrain endured twenty minutes of polite small talk and cups of over-brewed coffee, before he and Dominic left. After the stultifying atmosphere of the office and the obsequious attentions of Mr. Pitt, Evrain craved fresh air. He pushed through the door with Dominic close on his heels. Outside on the rain-slicked pavement, they looked at each other and shared a smile but then some of the tension returned, the atmosphere shifting like the calm before a storm.

"I'm so glad to be out of there. I couldn't breathe," Dominic said.

"I know exactly what you mean. That man sucks all the oxygen out of the air, I swear."

"Definitely creepy. I just want to go home. Take a shower."

"How did you get here?" Evrain asked Dominic before he could make some excuse and disappear. "Have you got your van?"

Dominic nodded. "It's parked just around the corner."

"Good. You can give me a lift back to the cabin. If I have to move in tonight, and apparently I do, I need to take a look around and decide what to bring from my apartment." He hoped that if he was decisive enough, Dominic wouldn't have the courage to question Evrain's right to tell him what to do.

"Okay, I can do that. I suppose a shower can wait."

"It can."

Evrain secretly hoped that Dominic would be happy to spend more time with him. They'd had little enough opportunity since Agatha's death. He made the most of the short walk to Dominic's parking spot, allowing his hand to occasionally brush against Dominic's as they strolled along. He caught several sideways glances and noticed Dominic chewing on his lower lip. His nerves were delicious. Evrain resisted the urge to hold hands, not because he was worried about reaction to a public display of affection, but because he knew that once he had Dominic in his grip he wouldn't be able to let go.

Dominic's truck was old but immaculately clean.

"It's not much, but it does the job." Dominic sounded apologetic as he unlocked the door. "Doesn't even have central locking." He shrugged.

"Well, you can afford something better now. It would be an investment in your business."

"Oh no, I couldn't," Dominic said. "She's a reliable old girl, I wouldn't just trade her in."

Evrain climbed into the cab and settled into the passenger seat. Inside, it smelled vaguely of moss and earth—a comforting scent of the countryside. Evrain breathed deeply, knowing the scent would forever remind him of Dominic.

"It's good to know you're so loyal." *Because once I make you mine, I'm never letting you go.*

Dominic slammed his door shut and settled in his seat. "Do you want to go home first and change?"

The question startled Evrain from his thoughts. He gave himself a once-over, catching Dominic's dubious glance. "Are you criticizing the way I look?" Evrain asked mischievously.

"No! I just thought..." Dominic stuttered into an unhappy silence. Evrain experienced guilt very rarely. This was one such time.

"I'm sorry, I'm being a dick." Evrain leaned across and placed a hand on Dominic's thigh. "You're right. This outfit isn't very practical, is it?"

Firm muscle clenched beneath his touch and Evrain was sorely tempted to see what would happen if he moved his fingers slightly higher. Wicked thoughts flashed through his mind and he grinned to himself before lifting his hand. There would be plenty of time for that and he'd scared Dominic enough for now. Grandmother dearest had done him a great favor by tying Dominic to him. He was going to enjoy reeling in those invisible cords, but he would take his time. Still, there was no harm in having a bit of fun in the meantime.

"Black suits you," Dominic whispered.

"Then I'll be sure to wear it more."

"Oh, I didn't mean..."

Evrain gave him a direct look. "I'm interested in what you enjoy, Dominic. What you appreciate. What turns you on."

"Stop it!" Dominic's words came out as a gasp. "Tell me where to go."

"And there it is." Evrain grinned. "I think that's what you enjoy the most. Me telling you what to do." He tapped one finger on his knee. "Me manhandling you probably comes a close second."

Dominic gripped the steering wheel tightly. He turned on the ignition. "Please, Evrain. Stop teasing me."

But it's so much fun! Evrain decided to be merciful. He gave directions to his apartment building then sat quietly while Dominic followed them. When they reached the entrance to the underground lot beneath Evrain's building, Evrain gave Dominic the guest code. Dominic drove down the ramp and pulled up in a vacant spot. He turned off the engine, which sputtered a little before cutting out completely.

"I can wait here." Dominic sounded hopeful.

"No, you won't, you'll come up with me. I'm not going to leave you sitting down here in the dark." Evrain used a challenging tone, daring Dominic to refuse him.

A small sigh signaled his victory. Evrain took it as an excellent sign for the future. Dominic was so clearly submissive it sent a thrill right to Evrain's core. He would make Dominic his own, and every small concession that Dominic made to Evrain's dominance was a step in the right direction.

They took the elevator to Evrain's apartment, soft music playing as they rose to the top floor. They were surrounded by mirrors, which allowed Evrain to watch Dominic's every movement. He had his hands shoved deep in his pockets and he shuffled from foot to foot as if unable to keep still.

"There's no need to be nervous," Evrain said as they reached their destination and the elevator doors slid open. "I apologize if I made you uncomfortable."

"Oh... It's not that. This place is just so..."

Evrain's block was luxurious to say the least. Dominic gazed at everything, taking in the plush carpets and artwork that decorated the hall.

"This is a really nice place," Dominic said.

"It is, but it's not mine," Evrain felt the need to clarify as he unlocked his front door. "It came with my job. I suppose I'll have to give it up now and commute from the cabin to the office. Hopefully the company will let me work from home a couple of days each week to save making the journey." He pushed open the door and led Dominic inside. "Make yourself at home, I won't be long." Evrain took off his jacket and threw it across a chair before heading for his bedroom. He stripped down to his underwear and rummaged in the wardrobe for an old pair of jeans. He was about to pull them on then smiled to himself, tossed them onto the bed then strolled back into the lounge instead.

"I should have said — the kitchen's through there, make yourself a drink if you'd like something." Evrain walked across the room and collected his discarded jacket.

Dominic's expression was priceless. He swallowed hard and blushed but didn't look away. Evrain observed Dominic's reaction to his state of undress with amusement. That creamy freckled skin did look very pretty with a light flush of color highlighting sharp cheekbones. He could feel himself becoming aroused and smirked as Dominic's discomfort increased. Dominic's gaze drifted downward, and Evrain had no doubt what it was fixed on.

"There are sodas in the fridge if you feel the need for something cool." Evrain waited a few more seconds then turned back into the bedroom. Let Dominic wonder what he was up to. Whatever his imagination conjured up wouldn't be too far from the truth.

Evrain shoved his shorts down and kicked them away. He strolled to the attached bathroom, his erection bouncing jauntily, begging for attention. Evrain wasn't one to deny himself. He fumbled in the bathroom cabinet for lube, coated his fingers in slick then tossed the tube away, not caring where it landed. He braced himself with one hand on the sink and took a tight grip of his aching shaft. He stared at his reflection in the mirror. His cheeks bore a hint of pink, his eyes were overly bright. As he jacked himself, his lips parted. His breath sped up. He visualized Dominic on his knees before him, luscious lips pressed around the head of his dick. He jerked his hand faster. His orgasm snuck up on him and a warm gush of fluid coated his palm. His muscles tensed and his throat chorded in a silent scream of release.

"Fuck, if he's that good when he's not even present, I can't wait until he's actually in the room." Evrain chuckled. It had been far too long since their brief but hot encounter in Dominic's tool shed. He was absolutely certain that soon, very soon, his daydreams would become reality again. Dominic belonged on his knees before him. The anticipation of the moment would only make the reality more spectacular.

Evrain cleaned himself up. He splashed some cool water on his cheeks in an effort to calm his heightened color, though he had no problem letting Dominic know that he'd done something about his arousal. Hopefully, it would leave Dominic frustrated and wanting. He retrieved his discarded jeans from the bed and pulled them on. The age-softened fabric caressed his ass and clung to his thighs. He shoved his bare feet into an old, paint-spattered pair of deck shoes, glad that he'd bothered to pack them. His mother had tried to toss them into the trash but he'd rescued them at the last moment and shoved them into the side of his suitcase. A faded university T-shirt under a woolen jumper made up the rest of his outfit. He grabbed the envelope that Angus Pitt had given him and went to find Dominic.

Evrain paused at his bedroom door. Dominic was in the corner of the room, bent over Evrain's work desk. Evrain took a moment to admire the lines of Dominic's body. Even beneath slightly baggy clothes, Dominic's lithe muscles were obvious. There was strength in his slender frame. The fabric of his pants pulled taut across his ass, making Evrain's mouth water.

"Mmm. Delicious."

Dominic startled at his words and spun around.

"Sorry, what did you say?"

"Nothing that was supposed to be out loud." Evrain smirked. "What do you think?"

"Of what?" Dominic blinked in confusion.

"My work. That *is* what you were looking at?"

"Oh, sorry… It was laid out here. I didn't mean to be nosy."

"It's not a problem. You're welcome to view it." Evrain's drawing table was covered with story layouts from a superhero comic strip that he was working on for an advertising campaign for a new aftershave, but peeking from beneath the sheets of paper was a hint of something else. He pulled the papers free and spread them out so that Dominic could see them. Dominic spent a moment absorbing the images. He gasped.

The black and white graphic showed a naked young man bound helplessly to his bed by creeping vines, tendrils of the plant curling around his cock and balls. His head was thrown back, his expression one of ecstasy.

"Does the image appeal to you?" Evrain stood at Dominic's shoulder and whispered close to his ear.

Dominic jumped. "I don't, I mean... Why would you think...?"

"It appeals to me, Dominic. That's why I drew it."

"He looks like me," Dominic murmured.

"He does, doesn't he? The likeness is remarkable." Evrain smirked. "There's good reason for that."

Dominic reached out, letting his fingertips brush the drawing. "It's so realistic. A couple of months ago I had a dream, well, a nightmare I suppose, and it was like this. It was the night after I met you at Aggie's for the first time."

Evrain froze. Could he somehow have influenced Dominic's dreams? He'd still been so new to his power that day—his emotions had been all over the place. *That's right, try to convince yourself it wasn't deliberate, Evrain.* He cupped the nape of Dominic's neck. "Was it a nightmare? Really? Are you sure it wasn't a fantasy made real?" Dominic's skin was warm and smooth to his touch.

"No, of course not!"

Dominic's fake indignation was amusing. Evrain massaged his neck, kneading away Dominic's tension. "There's no need to be embarrassed, Dominic. We all have fantasies and kinks. Perhaps you are just discovering yours."

Dominic leaned into his touch. A little moan escaped his lips. "It was so real. Scary but amazing."

Evrain threaded his fingers through Dominic's hair and pressed a light kiss to the side of his neck. "Then perhaps it *was* real."

Dominic pulled away and stared at him, wide-eyed. "What are you talking about? It couldn't have been real."

Evrain gave him a lazy smile. "No, of course not. Now, we should go, don't you think? There's a lot to get done." He didn't wait for a response, just moved toward the door. "If I wear you out enough, perhaps your dreams tonight will be just as...stimulating."

Chapter Nine

All the light and laughter that had surrounded Agatha's cabin had gone, or so it seemed to Evrain as he and Dominic walked down the path toward the rustic building. Storm clouds loomed, promising rain.

"I still can't believe she's not around anymore," Dominic said. "Have the police told you anything more about how the investigation is going?"

On the drive from Portland, Dominic had barely spoken a word, so Evrain welcomed the question, difficult though it was. He understood that Dominic had cared about Agatha just as much as he had.

"No, I haven't heard anything new. The investigating detective, O'Shea, gives me a courtesy call every now and again, but I doubt they will catch anyone. The trail's gone cold by now and they don't seem to have any leads to go on at all." Evrain's tone was sharper than he had intended. "Sorry, talking about it just gets me frustrated and angry." This was his first visit to the cabin since his grandmother's funeral and the memories of discovering her body were still horrifyingly fresh.

"I thought she was just sleeping when I found her." He paused on the path, kicking at fallen leaves. "I'd brought her shopping as usual. I wandered around, unpacking, talking to her. She didn't answer and I assumed she'd dozed off. Normally she'd be telling me off about something less than five minutes after I arrived. When she didn't stir, I went to check on her but she was gone." He began to walk again. "She was an old lady, she should have died peacefully in her sleep. Instead she had this expression on her face." He shuddered. "It was just awful." There was no need to share the gruesome details with Dominic.

"It must have been a terrible shock," Dominic said.

"It was if the world slowed down for a moment. I suppose it didn't sink in straight away that she'd been murdered, but I should have realized immediately. She was fit and healthy. Even at her age there was no reason for her to die so suddenly."

"She kept up with me in the garden just fine," Dominic agreed. "She was in great shape."

"After that, seeing her face, everything's a blur. Calling the police, waiting for them to arrive—which seemed to take forever—and then the endless questions."

They reached the garden gate. Dominic pushed it open and they approached the cabin door together.

"And of course they suspected me."

Dominic's eyes widened. "Why on earth would they do that?"

"I think close relatives are always the first port of call when it comes to suspects. I don't blame them at all— they were just doing their jobs. Once the medical examiner confirmed the time of death and I was able to provide rock-solid alibis, they left me alone."

"They spoke to me too," Dominic said. "But I'd been so busy I hadn't seen her for a couple of days, and, fortunately, I had plenty of witnesses to my whereabouts at the time of her death because I'd been redoing the window troughs outside the library. I do wonder, though, if I'd called in that evening, would I have been able to save her?"

"Or ended up dead yourself?" Evrain said. "Believe me, I've been through all the 'what if?'s. Someone wanted her dead and neither you nor I could have been with her twenty-four hours a day. A determined person would have got to her sooner or later." He pushed open the door.

Inside the cabin, everything was exactly the same as it had been weeks earlier. Evrain could picture his grandmother sitting in her usual chair, scolding him for some minor infraction. He wandered around touching things, letting his fingers absorb what was left of her presence. It provided a measure of comfort.

"I'll light a fire, shall I?" Dominic asked, moving toward the hearth.

Evrain felt the chill for the first time. "Good idea, it's cold in here."

Dominic scooped ash from the grate using a small brass shovel that Agatha kept nearby just for that purpose, depositing the waste in a copper bucket. He scrunched up some newspaper to line the grate, then added some kindling from the wood basket. Everything was very dry and caught well when he touched a match to the paper. He quickly added bigger pieces of wood and finally a couple of chunky logs. Soon a toasty blaze was roaring away.

Evrain took one of the armchairs next to the fire, and, after making sure that the flames were well established, Dominic sat in the other. An awkward silence followed, broken only by the crackle of burning wood.

Evrain took a deep breath. "I suppose we should open our letters and see what Grandmother has to say for herself," Evrain said, feeling strangely nervous.

Dominic nodded. He turned his envelope over and over in his hands. "Okay. You first."

Evrain ripped open his envelope, extracted the note from inside, then began to read. He chuckled. "It seems you have to hear this too."

He cleared his throat and began to read aloud, "Dearest Evrain, that you are reading this note means that I am gone earlier than I hoped and the challenges ahead of you have consequently increased. Mr. Pitt—and, yes, I know what impression he makes, but he is a good man and someone you can trust—should have told you to open this when you and Dominic are together. I hope, for once, you've obeyed instructions. You must read your letter aloud in Dominic's presence. He should then do the same." Evrain rolled his eyes. "Still telling me what to do, even from beyond the grave."

Dominic giggled. The sound went straight to Evrain's heart.

"I hope you will follow my wishes and move to the cabin immediately. You're a stubborn boy but it's for your own good. The cabin is warded and will provide a measure of protection for both you and Dominic while you learn to master your craft."

"Wait, does that mean what I think it does?" Dominic asked. "She wants us to move in together?" The pitch of his voice rose. "And what is she talking about? What wards, what craft?"

"Don't worry about that for a minute. Looks like she wants us to be housemates," Evrain replied. He waved his letter. "Let's see what else she has to say." He carried on reading. "Be diligent in continuing your training. Self-discipline is vital—I have shown you how to proceed, now it is up to you.

"My dear, you have enormous talent, but it will only truly mature once you can channel through a life partner. I have done what I can to set you on the right path in this but you can only follow your heart. You will never be an easy person to love—recognize that in yourself and it will help because I know you have it in you to love the right man deeply.

"There are those who would seek to harm you or to use your gifts for evil. Be vigilant. Protect yourself and the one you will come to love. I know that you will fulfill my expectations and be all that you can be. My spirit will be watching over you. Grandma."

Evrain looked up and met Dominic's questioning gaze. Tiny flashes of orange reflected in Dominic's blue eyes as the fire blazed in response to Evrain's emotional state.

"What is she talking about, Evrain?" Dominic asked.

"Why don't you read your letter, then everything might become clearer?" Evrain really hoped that Aggie would do the explaining for him.

Fingers trembling, Dominic broke the wax seal on the envelope and pulled out his own letter. It began in a similar way to Evrain's, instructing him to read it aloud.

"Dearest Dominic, I'm sure that you have known, or suspected, for some time that I am, or should I say *was*, a witch. I could see the knowledge in those beautiful eyes, but you were always too shy to ask. I am glad you were able to accept me and hope that you have learned from me."

Dominic stopped reading.

"It's true," Evrain said. "You knew it, just like she said."

"I suppose I did." Dominic lifted the letter again. "The talent runs deep in my family—my grandson possesses more power than I could ever have dreamed of. Evrain is the first warlock to be born to my family line in several hundred years." Dominic's eyes widened but he carried on reading, "For his own protection, he only gained full access to his abilities on his twenty-first birthday. The two of you are close in age so I'm sure you can understand a little of what he is going through. Powerful warlocks control their power by channeling some of their emotional energy through a life partner. This can only be achieved consensually and through a bond of love. I will not deceive you, Dominic, channeling is very painful. A relationship with a warlock is not to be taken lightly.

"You are bright enough to realize by now that I saw you as a potential partner for Evrain and that I planned to bring you together. Your quiet strength will provide the perfect counterpoint to his assertive confidence. Forgive me for putting you in this position, just promise me that you will think about my words before you make any decisions.

"However the future unfolds, I know that you will make good use of the land I have willed you. Do with it as you see fit, with my blessing. With much love, Agatha."

Dominic leaned back in his chair, staring at the piece of paper in his hand. "You have got to be kidding me. Did you slip something in my coffee back at the solicitor's?"

Evrain just sat and looked at him implacably.

"It can't be true. This is the real world, warlocks don't exist." He stood up and ran agitated fingers through his hair. "A witch I can handle. Aggie was great with remedies, that kind of thing. If that's witchcraft, then fine, who am I to judge? But a warlock? Jesus, I've stepped into a bad B-movie."

Evrain twisted his fingers into the required shape, made a gesture and the fire flared brightly next to them.

"No... I don't believe it. This is madness." Dominic got up. He backed to the door and opened it. Outside the rain was coming down in sheets.

Evrain made another gesture and a gust of wind slammed it closed again.

"It's true, Dominic. I realize it's a lot to take in and I don't blame you for being skeptical. I can't help what I am, but I'm sorry if that scares you. Leave if you wish, I won't try to stop you." He sighed as Dominic reopened the door and edged out into the cold. "It sounds like an old woman's ramblings, believe me I know," he whispered the words at the dancing flames and settled back to wait.

Outside Dominic turned his face to the sky and let the raindrops spatter against his skin in an attempt to clear his head. He walked to the back of the cabin, to the potting shed where he kept all his tools and gardening kit. He changed into an old pair of wellington boots that he stored there, tucking his jeans inside them. He grabbed a spade, then strolled to the vegetable patch and methodically began to dig over the ground. Several sections were planted and had been sadly neglected for the past few weeks. Turning the soil between the rows of growth was necessary work with all the weeds that had sprouted.

He let the contents of the two letters drift through his mind as the spade cut through the loamy earth. Deep down, he knew that Aggie wouldn't lie. She'd been sharp as a tack and scrupulously honest. It was just so hard to accept. And she thought that he and Evrain could be together? That was even more unbelievable than the whole witches and warlocks scenario. Evrain was charismatic, beautiful and talented. What possible use could he have for a lowly gardener? Sure, they'd had a few moments where Dominic's hopes had been raised, including one particularly astounding blow job, but that was it. Dominic had been too scared to risk his feelings any further.

Dominic dug until his muscles screamed at him to stop then dug some more. He could lose himself in the repetitive action of push, stamp and turn, ignoring the ache in arms and back. The rain got steadily harder and he was soaked to the skin before he finally paused. His thin shirt was plastered to his body, clinging uncomfortably to his skin. Rivulets of water ran down his face from strands of sodden hair. Absently he noticed the blisters on his hands where he had neglected to wear any gloves and shivered as his body temperature cooled. He abandoned the spade and walked slowly back to the house. He kicked off soaked boots before pushing the door open. He stood inside on the mat and shook as a puddle gathered around his feet.

Evrain took one look and swore. "Oh, for fuck's sake, what have you done to yourself? Get over here by the fire."

Dominic complied without resistance and steam began to hiss from his jeans as intense heat penetrated the cold, wet denim. The door slammed shut behind him. On its own.

"Strip." Evrain barked the order.

Dominic gave Evrain a startled glance at the perfunctory command. "What? No!"

"You need to get out of those wet clothes before you catch pneumonia, Dominic, so strip or I'll do it for you." Evrain advanced toward him.

Dominic discovered that his fingers were shaking so much from the cold that he was unable to undo his own shirt buttons. Evrain stepped right into his personal space with an exasperated hiss and deftly undid them all. He peeled the fabric away from Dominic's clammy skin and hung the soggy garment on the arm of the chair closest to the fire. Next he tackled Dominic's belt, undoing the buckle and slipping it from its loops.

"I should use this to tie you down so that you can't run away while I talk some sense into you." He undid Dominic's jeans then pulled them down to reveal snug black underwear that was also soaked through. "Were you testing the whole 'soaked to the skin' thing? These need to come off too." Evrain twanged the elastic. "I'll fetch a towel."

Dominic stood and shivered miserably. He hurt everywhere. Evrain was gone barely two minutes, before returning with a couple of thick towels.

"You know, this isn't what I had in mind when I imagined undressing you for the first time." Evrain stood and stared. "You have an amazing body." He threw one of the towels around Dominic's shoulders.

Dominic pulled it close. He had no idea what to say, and even if he did, his teeth were chattering too hard.

"I believe I told you to take off your underwear."

God he was bossy in the most appealing way. He stood there, hands on hips, waiting expectantly to be obeyed. Dominic guessed that if he didn't do as he'd been told, Evrain would feel obliged to help. Dominic was in too delicate a state to deal with Evrain's hands on his body so he slid his trunks down then stepped out of them, clutching the towel around himself defensively.

Evrain took the second towel and began to rub Dominic's limbs roughly, generating heat through the friction.

"Now's not the time to be shy, and besides, I know you have all the same parts I do. You weren't so reserved that day back at the diner. I need to get your circulation going, you must be virtually hypothermic. What the hell did you think you were doing out there?"

"I'm sorry," Dominic apologized through chattering teeth. "I just needed a bit of time to think."

"And you had to do that in the cold and rain? Idiot!" Evrain scolded.

Dominic hung his head and shook miserably — there wasn't much he could say and he didn't have the strength to defend himself. Evrain was right, he shouldn't have stayed outside so long, but surely he was due a bit of credit after all the revelations that had been dumped on him? Revelations he still wasn't sure he believed.

"I'm going to put you to bed so you warm through properly," Evrain said. "You'll have to stay here tonight. Do you think you can manage the stairs?"

Dominic's head was spinning, he couldn't articulate a sensible response so he kept his mouth shut. Evrain no doubt took the lack of an answer for agreement and manhandled him up the narrow staircase. If it hadn't been for Evrain propping him up from behind, Dominic thought he might have taken a tumble back down the stairs. He was so cold that even the hearthrug seemed like an attractive prospect. If he did fall, he could just curl up there in front of the fire.

The guest room turned out to be a far preferable option. Small but cozy, the double bed was covered in a heavy patchwork quilt. Evrain pulled it back and gestured in the direction of the bed.

"It's probably a bit dusty but the sheets are clean. Get in before you freeze to death. I'm going to see if I can find a hot water bottle. Grandmother didn't believe in electric blankets."

He turned away, and Dominic dropped his towel to climb under the covers. As he snuggled beneath the sheets, he realized that Evrain was staring into the dressing-table mirror. A mirror that would have given him a perfect view of Dominic's bare ass as he scrambled into bed. Evrain grinned, then winked, confirming that he'd enjoyed the view. Dominic hid his head beneath the covers and groaned.

Evrain left the bedroom door open a crack. He crossed the landing to the bathroom where he rummaged in the cupboard under the sink, letting out a small cry of victory when he discovered an ancient rubber bottle. He checked the stopper and there was no sign that the seal was perished. It would do the job. He took the bottle down to the kitchen where he could warm up a pan of water on the stove. A quick twist of his fingers had it bubbling away merrily in no time. Evrain filled the bottle, tested the stopper by giving the bottle a good shake, then took it back upstairs only to find that Dominic had already fallen asleep.

With all the worry lines smoothed from his face, Dominic appeared much younger. There were only six months between them but Evrain felt that he'd aged significantly since his twenty-first birthday. The knowledge of his heritage had come with a heavy weight of responsibility. He lifted the bed covers just enough to shove the hot water bottle into position near Dominic's feet then made sure that they were pulled up enough to cover his bare shoulders. Dominic's damp hair was curling a little at the ends and his lips were slightly parted, his breathing steady. As Evrain watched over the younger man, he felt incredibly protective. It would be so easy to lift the covers and have a really good look at Dominic's naked body. If the promise of that ass he'd glimpsed in the mirror was anything to go by, he knew he wouldn't be disappointed. He couldn't do it, though. He wanted Dominic to be fully aware of what was going on when Evrain did eventually get to touch again.

Reluctantly, Evrain left Dominic sleeping. He investigated the cabin, poking into all the cupboards, checking on supplies. As a child he'd often thought that the cabin was a kind of TARDIS, bigger on the inside than it seemed from the outside. Knowing what he did now about his grandmother, there was probably a good *Doctor Who* plotline in there somewhere. He could picture Agatha and the Doctor having polite conversation over herbal tea and cookies. Evrain sniggered as he explored and wondered if Dominic was a sci-fi fan.

He didn't venture into the attic for fear of disturbing Dominic's rest, but he did decide to turn the third bedroom into an office. Tomorrow he would bring a few things from home and set up his workstation. Hopefully Dominic could be persuaded to loan both his truck and his muscles to help with the removal process.

Evrain found clean sheets and blankets in the linen cupboard. He wiped off the layer of dust on the furniture in the master bedroom, then made up the bed. Much as he would have enjoyed a snuggle session with Dominic, he wouldn't presume that Dominic would be prepared to take the next step just yet, if ever. He still had to come to terms with the whole warlock thing and that might take a while.

Evrain turned on the central heating and gave the bathroom a quick wipe-over. Four weeks' worth of dust lay over everything but it didn't take long to clean up. Aggie had a glorious, claw-footed tub that he couldn't wait to try out. A soak in the bath would have to wait for a while, though—there was a bit more exploration to complete first.

Downstairs was one huge open-plan space and would take a bit more effort to clean. That could wait. He investigated the freezer, which proved to be well stocked, and extracted a plastic tub of frozen stew to heat on the stove. For tonight, they could manage with what was at the cabin. There were plenty of tins in the cupboards and one night without fresh produce wouldn't kill them.

It was seven o'clock when Evrain detected the sounds of stirring from upstairs. Dominic had slept for about three hours. Evrain loaded up a tray with bowls of stew, a couple of forks and mugs of tea. Fresh bread to go with the stew would have been nice. He wondered if Dominic knew how to bake. He headed for the guest room. He pushed open the door with his ass and reversed into the room, then rotated and almost dropped the tray. Dominic was sitting up in bed, bare-chested, hair tousled from sleep, blue eyes blinking in confusion. To Evrain he looked young, vulnerable and incredibly desirable. Evrain's heart beat just a little faster as he was rewarded with a shy, tentative smile. He bent to put the tray on the edge of the bed, then held out one of the bowls and a fork to Dominic.

"This is stew. It's not poisoned. Eye of newt and tongue of bat were not involved in its construction, at least I don't think so — I got it out of the freezer. So eat it while it's hot."

Dominic took the bowl and obediently spooned some of the savory dish into his mouth.

"It's great. Thank you, I'm starving."

Evrain grunted. "It's early evening — you didn't get lunch." He placed the mugs of tea on the bedside table, careful to put them on a mat to avoid marking the wood. He shifted the tray onto the floor, then made himself comfortable at the end of the bed. He began to eat his own meal and took the opportunity to steal another glance at Dominic. Dark red hair flickered copper in the light of the one small lamp and Dominic's eyes seemed to gleam from within, like sapphires. The beginnings of stubble shadowed his jaw and upper lip, and Evrain wondered what it would feel like grazing his own sensitive skin. Dominic had a sharp, aquiline nose and a tiny birthmark, shaped like a star, high on one cheekbone.

Suddenly he realized that Dominic was staring right back at him.

"I can see a lot of Aggie in you, she must have been a great beauty in her youth," Dominic said. He ducked his head as if realizing that he had unintentionally complimented Evrain as well as his grandmother.

"Thank you. So you can see past what I am, Dominic. Just a man, not a monster?"

Dominic's lashes fluttered. He took another spoonful of stew, chewed then swallowed. "I see a mystery. A man, but something else, something I don't understand."

Evrain put his bowl down. He grasped Dominic's wrist in a firm grip. "You don't have to be afraid of me. I promise."

"But I *am* afraid, Evrain. Regardless of what you say you are, I'm terrified of the way you make me feel and that has absolutely nothing to do with the supernatural." His voice was so soft that it barely registered, but he didn't pull away from Evrain's grasp.

Evrain just smiled, released him and carried on eating. When they were both finished, he loaded the tray with their crockery and stood up.

"Get some sleep. You need to rest. This has been an emotional day and I don't think we should carry on this conversation until the morning."

"You don't?" Dominic's pout was adorable.

Evrain resisted the temptation to take that sweet lower lip between his teeth and give it a punishing nip.

"I don't, because if I stay in this room any longer I won't be able to control myself, and much as I'm looking forward to fucking you through the mattress very soon, now is not the time."

"Oh!" Dominic managed shocked innocence so well.

It made Evrain even harder than he already was. If the tent in the bedclothes was anything to go by, Dominic was equally aroused by their conversation.

Evrain grabbed the laden tray and retreated. Back in the kitchen, he put the tray down and leaned against the sink, digging his nails into the palms of his hands. Resisting the temptation to bruise those soft, sensuous lips had been close to impossible and his cock was not amused at his willpower. He sat by the fire and tried to calm his thoughts. The flames were spitting and sparking, mirroring his agitation as he unzipped his fly and allowed his aching cock some freedom. He gripped the arms of the chair hard and closed his eyes. With Dominic so close to him, he found it easy to focus. Light wisps of breeze caressed him, spiraling around his rigid cock with tantalizing delicacy. Heated fingers of air squeezed and released in time with his pulse and as his heartbeat quickened so did they. The soft touches were torture, and eventually Evrain gave in to his own need and grasped himself firmly. In the hearth, the fire rose and fell in time with his movements until finally there was a crackling explosion of smoke and flame as he came with a strangled moan.

"Oh God, that's so good." There had to be some benefit to being a powerful warlock. If he had to settle for magical masturbation then that might just be enough.

Happily sated, Evrain had a wicked thought. He washed his hands, then crept up the stairs as quietly as the creaky old boards would allow. He stood at the door to the guest bedroom and pushed it open just far enough that he could see Dominic lying in bed. His eyes were closed, the lashes fluttering against his cheeks. *Fuck, he's so beautiful. I could jack off to that image quite happily.* But that wasn't why Evrain was lurking outside Dominic's door. The tiniest pang of guilt hit him, but he brushed it away. *I need the practice. This benefits both of us.* He began to twist his fingers into intricate shapes.

Dominic's eyes snapped open, his lips parted in a silent gasp. Evrain had to bite his lip to stop a chuckle escaping. He flicked his fingers and sent spikes of heat toward the bed.

"Oh!" Dominic whimpered, the sound one of pleasure rather than fear. He rolled onto his stomach then kicked at the bed covers until they slipped to midthigh.

Evrain licked his lips. He directed his warm spears at Dominic's exposed ass, probing, penetrating just as he might have done with his fingers given the chance.

Dominic stretched his arms over his head and gripped the rail of the headboard. Face down, it seemed to Evrain that Dominic had his teeth embedded in his pillow. He was holding the metal headboard so tightly that his knuckles bleached. Evrain sent licks of heat to brush Dominic's skin, slowly moving closer to his virgin entrance, pushing apart his creamy cheeks. He applied gentle pressure to the small of Dominic's back, holding him firmly in place, and increased the heat. It was nowhere near hot enough to burn, but Dominic would feel every touch.

Dominic gasped and spread his legs wide in wanton abandon. He wasn't attempting to escape—rather he seemed to have given in to sensation. He drew up his knees, sticking his ass in the air, and Evrain took up the invitation eagerly. He filled Dominic's channel with pulsating waves of warmth. There would be no pain, just a tingling pleasure spreading inside Dominic's body. Evrain's fingers moved almost of their own accord, faster and faster. Dominic groped for his cock and managed to take hold. He'd barely made contact when he came, producing streams of creamy cum with a hiss of pleasure.

Once his body was drained, Dominic rolled onto his back and stared blindly at the ceiling. He appeared emotionally and physically exhausted. Evrain could only imagine the terrifying exhilaration of giving in to something he didn't understand. He froze in place, determined not to give away his presence.

"Hell fire, Evrain, are you trying to kill me with pleasure?" Dominic muttered.

Evrain choked back a laugh. He was so busted. Dominic might not have seen him but he knew he was involved. Evrain couldn't wait to tease Dominic the next morning and make it clear that he was guilty as charged.

Chapter Ten

The next day, Saturday, dawned with the threat of more rain. The sky seemed to boil with dark, rolling clouds tumbled by the gusty wind. Evrain's mood always seemed to reflect the weather, or perhaps it was the other way round. He'd slept badly, something he put down to spending the night in his grandmother's bed. He felt unsettled and impatient, his thoughts a jumble of confused images. He needed to vent but hadn't yet explained the process to Dominic. *The poor love's freaked out enough as it is.*

Evrain paced around while Dominic pulled together a makeshift breakfast of honey-sweetened porridge and herbal tea, then sat and drummed his fingers on the table as he waited to be served. Dominic brought everything to the table and set a steaming bowl in front of Evrain.

"I don't know what's it's going to taste like—I'd normally make it with milk rather than water." He took the seat next to Evrain.

"Thanks, I'm sure it will be fine." Evrain dipped his spoon in the viscous mixture and gave it a stir. "I'll get groceries later."

"You'll need to bring all your things over from Portland, won't you?" Dominic asked.

"Yep, and you must have things you want to move too."

"Oh, I'm not sure that's necessary, is it? Aggie didn't specify that I had to move in here, it was just a suggestion."

"A suggestion that you will follow," Evrain said, unblinking.

"But you can't tell me what to do, Evrain." Dominic's voice shook a little as he said the words, as if he didn't quite believe them.

"Oh, I think I can." Evrain stroked Dominic's thigh beneath the table, enjoying the jerk of muscles. "Did you sleep well last night? Any interesting dreams?"

Dominic's spoon clattered into his bowl. "That was you, wasn't it? You did those things to me."

"Now how could that be the case?" Evrain said with a smirk. "You don't believe I'm a warlock."

Dominic's cheeks colored. "Then how do you know what I'm talking about?"

"Ah, you've caught me. I must say it was delicious watching you squirm. How did it feel, those fingers of heat and air assaulting you, holding you down?"

"You bastard!" Dominic shoved his chair back, escaping Evrain's touch. "Why would I want to move in here with you, when you do things to me without my permission?"

Evrain chuckled. "Oh, save the false indignation for someone who cares. You loved every second of it and all it would have taken for me to stop was one word.

One word. If you'd said no, or indicated in any way that you weren't into it, I would have stopped immediately." He tapped his fingers on the table. "Perhaps we should agree on a safeword for you?"

Dominic's eyes widened. "What? Why would I need a safeword? Are you into bondage and...and whipping and stuff?"

"What do you think?" Evrain teased.

"I don't know what to think. You confuse the hell out of me."

"Good. You can think about your safeword while you're at work today. You do have to work, don't you?"

Dominic nodded. "This morning. I have two jobs in White Salmon. I should be finished by lunchtime. You didn't answer my question."

"No, I didn't, did I?" Evrain grinned. "I'm sure you'll have great fun letting your imagination run riot, though. If you're very good, I may give you a proper answer later. And who the hell names a place after a fish?"

"God, could you be any more annoying?"

"I could try." Evrain smiled sweetly.

"I give up." Dominic piled the dirty dishes in the sink. "I can take you back to Portland before I start, if you want to go home."

"This is home now, whether I like it or not." Evrain sipped his tea thoughtfully. "I can wait until you've finished. There's loads to do here and if you're finished by lunchtime, we'll still have plenty of time to move my things over and then yours later on."

Dominic growled. He actually growled, though the noise was more like a puppy practicing than a pissed-off Rottweiler.

"I have *not* agreed to move in here."

"You don't need to agree, you just need to do as you're told. You'll find it makes our relationship a whole lot easier." Evrain smiled, knowing it would annoy Dominic even more.

"We have a relationship?" Dominic sighed. "No, don't answer that. I don't think I'm ready for whatever you might say. I have to get to work."

"You do that, sweetheart." Evrain raised his mug in a toast. "We'll talk again later. You have a good day."

* * * *

After calling in to his apartment to change into his work clothes, Dominic applied himself to his jobs with his usual dedication but found that hard physical work was not enough of a distraction to keep his thoughts away from Evrain. As he mowed the huge lawns of one of his regular customers, he had too much time to think. So long as he steered the ride-on mower in a reasonably straight line, it didn't require much attention.

He put aside the idea that Evrain was something more than human – he was having a hard enough time coping with the idea that the attraction between them was apparently mutual without having to deal with magic and mayhem. Whatever had happened the previous evening, it could be put down to exhaustion, an overactive imagination, hallucinations brought on by stress and the shock of inheriting so much wealth from Agatha. There had to be a rational explanation for all the strangeness. Fires flared all the time. Doors slammed on their own – a simple gust of wind could cause that.

Their conversation that morning had confused Dominic even more. Evrain was so sure of himself. He dropped hints about being into a BDSM lifestyle, something that both scared and excited Dominic.

"Safeword! He wants me to choose a safeword!" Dominic shouted at a passing wood pigeon. He supposed there was no harm in thinking of a suitable word. He'd done enough Internet research to have heard about the traffic light system, but red, yellow, green didn't float his boat. He needed a word that would irritate Evrain. That would make thinking one up worthwhile. Dominic hummed as he turned the mower for another pass over the neatly cropped grass. He had just the word.

Dominic couldn't imagine taking the initiative to move things along with Evrain. He got so tongue-tied around him—it was even worse than usual and that was saying something. He'd always been shy—it was part of his defense mechanism not to attract attention that had, too often in the past, turned to aggression. In his late teens there had been a couple of older boys at his group home that had attempted to force him to suck them off, holding him down, wrenching his hair and hitting him when he'd resisted. They hadn't succeeded due to a timely interruption from a member of staff, but the experience had taught Dominic a valuable lesson in remaining inconspicuous.

As he'd gotten older he had eventually realized that men found him attractive but no one had ever appealed to him enough to gain his trust. Evrain's magnetism was breaking down his barriers—he just hoped that he would have the courage to respond if Evrain tried to take things further between them. The incident in the tool shed had been spur of the moment. A one-off. It had been easy to drop to his knees in the darkness, and that brief pleasure had fueled his fantasies ever since.

He had thought last night that Evrain was about to make a move, but then he had withdrawn. It had been a relief but disappointing at the same time. Evrain had said he wanted to fuck Dominic through the mattress. Dominic suspected he'd be quite happy to go along with that suggestion.

He was still trying to make sense of his feelings but physically his body was beginning to overrule his mind. Evrain would only have to issue one of his infuriating commands and Dominic would fold like a poorly constructed house of cards. He glanced at his watch for the third time in fifteen minutes and grinned ruefully. Clock watching was a bad habit to get into, but he could almost feel the pull of whatever invisible tether connected him to Evrain.

Dominic got back to the cabin much later than he'd planned. He had been delayed by having to collect a part for a misbehaving hedge trimmer, which had had to be fixed before he could complete his second job of the morning. Then he'd gone home to pack an overnight bag and fill a cooler with a few essentials. He'd skipped lunch, but it was still almost two o'clock when he walked back down the garden path to Agatha's cabin. The butterflies engaged in formation-flying in his stomach were making him feel a bit queasy and he hesitated outside the door. He looked at his mud-stained work trousers and worn shirt and sighed. His hands were engrained with dirt and yesterday's blisters concealed beneath ragged bandages wound around his palms. He desperately needed a shower and wished that he could have cleaned up before seeing Evrain again, but there was no time.

In front of him, the door swung silently open.

"Are you going to stand out there all day, or are you coming inside?" Evrain's voice came from somewhere inside.

Dominic didn't allow himself to think about how Evrain had known he was there, or how he had opened the door without being anywhere near it. He swallowed and went in. The door slammed shut behind him. Dominic dropped his bag and put the cooler down.

Evrain sat, cross-legged, on the rug in front of the fire, surrounded by an assortment of jars and bottles containing all manner of herbs and liquids. He had a smudge of dirt across his cheek and still managed to pull off effortless beauty.

"You're late."

Dominic wasn't fooled by Evrain's calm tone. His statement held undertones of annoyance and his strange eyes glinted as he looked up.

"Sorry." Dominic instinctively knew that defending himself was pointless. Even though Evrain had no right to reprimand him, he found his body responding to the curt tone. Evrain stood and approached him. He moved with sinuous grace, a wild animal stalking its prey.

"I don't like to be kept waiting."

Dominic took a nervous step backward, then another until the door halted his retreat. He froze as Evrain moved closer.

"You've been a big problem for me today, Dominic. I've been…distracted. I couldn't settle to any of the jobs I needed to do because I kept slipping into daydreams about all the things I would like to do to you instead."

Dominic swallowed and pressed against the solid wood behind him.

"The question is, will you let me?" Evrain seemed to be talking to himself as much as to Dominic. "I suspect there may have been bad experiences in your past. I'm pretty sure you're a virgin, but you seem to be sending the right signals. It's not in me to pretend to be something I'm not, I'll just have to make it clear what I want from you and see what reaction I can provoke."

Dominic's mouth was as dry as dust. His cock rose, pressing hard against his zipper. He felt for the door handle.

"Trying to run away again?" Evrain reached forward and stroked Dominic's face with a finger. "I think we need to break that habit, don't you?"

He grabbed Dominic's wrists and pushed them roughly back against the wood at shoulder height, muttering under his breath as he did. The grain shifted and the wood seemed to bulge outward, growing two small branches that twisted around Dominic's wrists then rooted themselves back into the door.

Dominic gasped. His head jerked from side to side as his mind attempted to assimilate what had happened. Evrain stood back and admired his handiwork, ignoring Dominic's futile attempts to get free.

"Stop struggling. It's a pointless waste of energy," Evrain snapped.

"How did you...? My God, it's true, isn't it? You really are a warlock."

"Ten out of ten for observation. Isn't that what I've been trying to convince you of? What Agatha told you? Perhaps this demonstration will finally get you to admit that there are things in this world that defy explanation."

"Let me go, Evrain." Dominic pulled against his wooden bonds until his wrists ached.

"You'll have bruises. I like the idea of my marks on you." Evrain ran one finger along the inside of Dominic's waistband and undid the button. "Did you do what I asked and decide on a safeword?"

"Stop!" Dominic twisted his hips.

"You see, that's why you need the safeword. I know you don't really want me to stop. With a safeword you can protest all you like but I'll just keep going. Use your safeword and everything ends. Immediately."

Dominic panted, his breath coming in rapid gasps. He couldn't get enough air into his lungs. "Salem! My safeword is Salem," he managed to get the word out.

"Oh, very droll." Evrain slowly pulled down Dominic's zipper. His cock sprang free. "You naughty boy. Going commando! I like it." Evrain raised one eyebrow and grinned as Dominic moaned in embarrassment.

"I didn't have any clean underwear with me to put on this morning. I don't tend to keep fresh shorts in my pocket, okay?" The cool air on his overheated flesh was torment. Dominic jerked his pelvis, seeking contact.

"I can't believe you're worried about that, considering the position you find yourself in. Though this" —Evrain gripped Dominic's rigid shaft firmly— "seems to suggest you rather enjoy being restrained."

Dominic thrust into Evrain's hand. He couldn't deny how turned on he was, it was patently obvious. When Evrain took his hand away, Dominic wanted to cry from frustration.

"Please…" He wasn't too proud to beg.

"Don't worry, I'm not done with you yet." Evrain's eyes gleamed. He grasped Dominic's pants and yanked them down to his ankles. "That's better."

He slid his hand up and down Dominic's dick until pre-cum slicked the head. When Evrain dropped to his knees, Dominic forgot how to breathe. He became capable of nothing more than needy moans and whimpers.

Evrain took a long, protracted lick. He swiped his tongue from the bulbous head of Dominic's cock all the way to the root.

"Fuck!" Dominic's thighs tensed and he pushed his ass away from the door as Evrain took him into his mouth and compressed his lips.

With one hand, Evrain fondled Dominic's balls, then he pushed a finger between Dominic's ass cheeks and probed at his entrance, all the time lathing Dominic's dick with a hot tongue.

When Evrain pulled away, Dominic sobbed. From his position on the floor, Evrain glanced up. "Would you like me to stop?"

"Please…"

"It's the last thing I want to do. Stop that is. You taste amazing, earthy and sweet at the same time."

Dominic shook his head frantically, he couldn't articulate what he wanted but he was desperate for Evrain to continue. He had a magical tongue, literally, though outside Dominic's strange bonds there was no hint of any spells at work. Dominic had never thought that being dominated this way would be such a turn-on, but despite being bound he felt less restrained than he ever had. He gave up all control.

"God, please…"

"My wish is your command." Evrain continued to suck and lap at him.

"Coming!" Dominic stuttered.

Evrain released him, and Dominic almost screamed. Evrain cocked his head to one side. "Well, just this once, I'll let you come without permission. But you need to understand that these are mine now." He took hold of Dominic's balls and gave them a firm squeeze. "So is this." He flicked the head of Dominic's cock with the tip of his tongue. "You'll only come when I allow it from now on."

At that moment, Dominic would have agreed to anything. He nodded. "Yes, yes... Please don't stop."

Evrain got back to work, sucking hard. Dominic thrust his groin forward but Evrain allowed him no control, he held all the power even on his knees. That thought pushed Dominic over the edge. His orgasm overcame him in a rush of heat and intense pleasure. Evrain didn't pull away. In fact he smiled as he swallowed everything that Dominic shot into his throat, then licked his lips.

Dominic sagged in his bonds. The wood around his wrists was the only thing keeping him upright.

"You are stunning like this, shocked by your own ecstasy." Evrain stood. He took Dominic's softening cock in his palm as if testing the weight. "Mine now. Don't forget."

He made a slight gesture with his free hand and the door reverted to its normal state. Dominic sagged against it. The gentle kiss that Evrain pressed to his lips was almost as shocking as the magic Dominic had witnessed. Evrain took a step back. Dominic gathered enough sense to pull up his pants. He massaged his wrists, rubbing at the soreness. Evrain gave him a contemplative look that had him fidgeting anxiously.

"I think you are going to enjoy being spellbound." Evrain smiled a wicked, knowing smile. "And as

Grandmother continually reminded me, I do need to get plenty of practice."

Dominic ducked his head. Just the thought of what 'spellbound' could mean was enough to have his dick straining to rise again. He had a feeling that it was going to be an enjoyably arduous afternoon.

Chapter Eleven

"Nobody has ever done that for me before," Dominic whispered. He closed his eyes and shivered at the memory of what Evrain had done to him. It was as if every nerve in his body had stored a recording of the sensation and needed little encouragement to replay the experience in his mind. He half expected a glib response from Evrain but instead he found himself drawn in for another kiss. "Thank you. For not making fun of me," he said when he had a moment to draw breath.

"Such innocent gratitude is something to be treasured," Evrain murmured. "And not something I've heard from a boyfriend before."

Dominic's heart pounded. "Boyfriend?"

"Well, of course. You don't think I'd do that for just anybody, do you? I'm not in the habit of publicizing my abilities to all and sundry."

"I suppose not. I'm still trying to suspend disbelief myself. It's a little hard to accept that what you can do isn't just a figment of my imagination."

"It's strange." Evrain circled him slowly, and Dominic had to fight the urge to follow him with his eyes. "I didn't discover the truth about myself until my twenty-first birthday. I've only been using the power for six months. I'm still a complete novice at this, yet when you are near, everything is more focused, more controlled. I couldn't even light a candle properly until that evening we met. Before that I had a tendency to blow things up." He dragged his hand across the back of Dominic's neck. "Why is that, do you think?"

At Evrain's touch, featherlight though it was, the downy hairs on the back of Dominic's neck stood on end. He had to concentrate before he could speak coherently. "I've no idea." His tongue tripped over even those three small words as Evrain continued his fingers' journey down Dominic's jaw line then across his lips. Standing face to face with Evrain once more, Dominic felt like he was drowning in the mysterious dark green depths of Evrain's eyes. His legs were weak and rubbery and his cock was fighting to escape the confines of his clothes.

Evrain cupped the nape of his neck with a cool hand and pulled him forward into the kind of searing, passionate kiss he'd thought existed only in romance novels. Organized thought was unmanageable. As it was, the heat of soft lips, the probing of a sweet tongue, became all-consuming and the need to think was irrelevant.

Evrain released him and he couldn't restrain a gasp. He wanted to beg to be taken, right there and then, in front of the fire. "I'd really like to do that again," he whispered, unable to prevent the slight tremor in his voice.

"Mmm." Evrain licked his lips and looked very pleased with himself. "I'd like that too. But perhaps you should go and take a shower first?"

Belatedly, Dominic remembered the state he was in and ran a hand through his hair. "Sorry. Yes, that might be a good idea. You muddle my brain. I must reek from working all morning."

"Not at all. You smell of the earth and freshly mown grass among other things. I love it. But you have mud in your hair and on your hands." Evrain took up both Dominic's hands, removed the ragged bandages and rubbed his thumbs across the palms. "Which are in danger of infection. I want you clean so that I can make you dirty again."

"Oh!" That sounded so good. "I'll just…" Evrain was blocking his route to the stairs and made no attempt to get out of his way. Dominic was forced to squeeze past him. Evrain twitched one dark eyebrow as Dominic's obvious arousal brushed against his hip.

"You have remarkable powers of recuperation," Evrain said. "No touching yourself in the shower other than to wash, and if you think I won't know if you do, you're wrong."

Dominic scampered up the stairs, ignoring Evrain's deep, throaty laugh. He gave thanks that Agatha had enjoyed small luxuries and had invested in a rain shower above her antique tub. He stripped off his work clothes, kicking them into a pile in the corner of the room, then climbed beneath the spray. Appreciative little noises came unbidden as heat penetrated his sore muscles.

To take his mind off Evrain, Dominic focused on lathering soap and shampoo into his body and hair. Aggie had made her own soaps, the thick cakes scented with petals and herbs. The slight abrasion helped clean the dirt from his skin and made him tingle. Once he was clean, Dominic reduced the temperature for a final cold blast that left him hopping from one foot to the other in his haste to find a warm towel. Other than the touch needed to wash, Dominic had been obedient to Evrain's order and not handled his cock. The chill of the water had softened his erection but as soon as he thought about being pinned to the door, it revived once more.

Cursing, he lifted the towel away from his groin. Even that slight friction was torment. He gave up and dropped it to the floor, standing naked before the sink. He found an unopened package of disposable razors and a shaving stick in the back of the bathroom cabinet. As he hadn't shaved that morning, he lathered up and carefully scraped the fine stubble from his chin.

He gave his reflection a critical examination. Familiar blue eyes stared back at him and he frowned, clinically assessing pale, freckled skin and lips that he had always felt were a little too feminine.

"What the hell does he see in me?" he whispered. He shook his head, a few droplets of water scattering from the ends of his hair. He had dreamed of submitting to another man ever since he'd been old enough to understand what submission was but he had never risked his feelings in this way before. Evrain was arrogant, assertive, but with just a hint of uncertainty beneath the bravado. Dominic suspected that Evrain was feeling his way just as much as he was. There wasn't that much difference between their ages after all, and Evrain was coping with a whole new world that

Dominic couldn't hope to understand. A relationship with him was going to be a risk, but Dominic was convinced it was a risk worth taking. That didn't make it any easier.

"And easy isn't worth having, that's what Aggie used to say." He hung his damp towel on the rail and scooped up his dirty clothes before padding back to the spare room. He was going to have to pay another visit home soon, if only to do some laundry and pick up some more fresh clothes. He extracted a clean set of clothes from his overnight bag, relieved that he had remembered to pack underwear. He pulled on a pair of clean, if faded, jeans and a dark green, brushed cotton shirt. Finger-combing his hair, he padded down the stairs barefoot and silent, the wood warm under his feet. He reached the curve in the staircase and froze. He could hear voices coming from the direction of the kitchen. Evrain hadn't mentioned expecting any visitors, but then why would he? He could easily have arranged something while Dominic had been out at work.

Dominic listened carefully through the light crackling of the fire. He could pick out Evrain's deep tones but the other voice he didn't recognize. He pressed close to the wall and moved quietly down a couple more steps, some instinct keeping him from introducing himself.

Evrain's guest wore a long leather coat and a felt hat with a blood red band. One gloved hand rested on the top of a silver-capped cane. Taller than Evrain and much broader, he filled the room with an ominous air. A long, blond plait reached partway down the visitor's back. Dominic was eager to see his face but held back.

Evrain moved into view. Briefly his eyes widened as he caught sight of Dominic then narrowed in a clear warning to stay concealed. Dominic complied with a silent step back but he didn't go far, he was too curious to hear what the two of them were talking about.

"Symeon, get to the point. I have things to do," Evrain snapped.

So this wasn't a welcome guest. Dominic was even more intrigued now he had a name.

"You would benefit from the guidance I can provide, boy." The blond-haired man's voice had a slight rasp to it, making him sound as if he had a sore throat. Despite his size, his voice wasn't that deep, but for some reason its timbre sent a chill the length of Dominic's spine. The cane tapped steadily on the floor.

"My grandmother did not agree." Evrain's voice was smooth and calm as if he were trying to delete any emotion from it. Dominic never wanted to be on the receiving end of that blank coldness.

"Your grandmother had old-fashioned values that have no place in the modern world," Symeon said. "You have great power, boy. You need to be schooled in how to use it and only another warlock can do that. There aren't many of us around to help you."

Dominic took a sharp intake of breath. Symeon was another warlock—presumably one with a lot more experience than Evrain.

"She believed we should use our abilities for the benefit of others, not just ourselves. Something I agree with."

Symeon's gloved fist clenched over the top of the cane, stretching the leather tight across his knuckles. "What is the point of power if you cannot use it for your own comfort? Agatha was living in the wrong century." His annoyance was clear in his abrupt tone.

"You and I are different, Evrain. Together we could be unstoppable."

"It might make me outmoded, Symeon, but I believe in my grandmother's philosophy. I have no desire for the kind of wealth and power you crave." Evrain moved, placing his body between Symeon and the stairs.

"You should take care, boy, you don't want me as an enemy."

Evrain sighed. "Please don't threaten me, Symeon. I have no intention of interfering in your business interests. Leave me alone and I will accord you the same consideration."

Symeon paced up and down. "I'm not sure that will be possible. Every time you use the power, the world reverberates with your strength and you haven't even begun to channel yet. You are a threat to my peace of mind and I don't like being threatened." He glanced around. "By the way, where is that gorgeous redhead of yours?"

"What are you talking about?"

"Your sweet little boyfriend. Don't be coy, I make it my business to know what you and your family are up to."

"He's none of your concern."

"So you haven't taken him yet?" That sounded like an accusation.

"That's hardly something I'd share with you. My private life is just that—private." Evrain's voice was rough with anger.

"Take good care of him, Evrain. I would hate for anything bad to happen to him."

Dominic's stomach knotted at the barely veiled threat. He had heard enough and crept back up the stairs. It proved to be a timely move as he heard Evrain maneuver his visitor toward the front door.

"Get out, Symeon. If you go anywhere near Dominic, if you so much as touch a hair on his head, I swear you will find out exactly how powerful I am."

Symeon laughed, a sound akin to nails scraping across a blackboard. "Goodbye, Evrain. We will meet again soon, I'm sure. Think about what I've said. I'm a far preferable ally than an enemy."

The fact that Evrain shut the door gently was even more telling than if he had slammed it with force. Dominic shot down the stairs and skidded to a halt in front of Evrain who was leaning back against the closed door. All color had bleached from his skin, making the strange green of his eyes stand out even more than usual.

"Are you okay? You don't look well." Dominic reached out and touched Evrain's arm. Evrain immediately clasped Dominic's hand in a firm grip.

"I'm fine now he's gone."

"Who was he, Evrain? Another warlock, obviously." Dominic allowed himself to be pulled into a hug.

"Someone I don't want you anywhere near." Evrain's voice was coldly furious and the words snapped out like the crack of a whip.

"I'm a grown-up—I make my own decisions." Dominic attempted to extract himself from Evrain's arms with no success.

"Not in this. He's dangerous. Stay away from him."

Dominic began to protest but Evrain stopped him with a kiss. He kissed him hard, encircling his waist with a strong arm and holding him close. It was so different from the kiss they had shared earlier. That had been a sensual exploration—this was rough, demanding and spoke of absolute possession. Dominic found himself responding as Evrain wound his fingers through Dominic's hair and tugged him even closer. Dominic parted his lips to allow Evrain entry, accepting the thrusts of his tongue willingly. Eventually Evrain loosened his grip and they pulled apart. Evrain slipped his hand downward from Dominic's waist to cup the curve of his ass.

"You're mine. Every beautiful inch of you. Symeon does not get to look at you in the wrong way, let alone touch you. Do you have a problem with that?"

"I... No, I don't think I do." Dominic raised his eyes timidly, his face heating. "But you have to be honest with me. I'll do what you say, but you have to tell me who he is and why he's dangerous."

"I don't want to scare you." Evrain frowned and pulled him into a secure embrace. "You are too important to me."

"I'm not some delicate flower that needs protecting. I can look after myself." He might not have magical powers but he wasn't completely useless.

"You sound offended. I admire your spirit." Evrain led him to the table and they both sat down. "I don't doubt your courage, Dominic, but you would have no defense against Symeon. He *is* a warlock, like me."

"Not at all like you from what I overheard," Dominic said. "Let me make a drink and then we can talk properly. I brought milk and fresh coffee back from home so we can have the good stuff."

Evrain's eyes lit up. "I love you. You are the perfect boyfriend."

It was a throwaway comment, but it still made Dominic's mouth go dry. He'd never been in love so he wasn't sure what he felt for Evrain but if love was tingling senses, a stomach full of knots and a sense of elation every time Evrain touched him, then he guessed he was a lost cause.

Dominic set up the fancy coffee machine, following Evrain's directions. He jumped a little when it began to spit and hiss.

"It's okay," Evrain chuckled. "That's normal. It always makes loads of noise as if producing a sublime brew is a battle for supremacy."

"If you say so." Dominic stood well back from the temperamental machine. When it finally went quiet apart from the gentle hiss of steam, he poured coffee, added milk then rejoined Evrain.

They sat at the table, which was scrubbed white with age, holding mugs of aromatic liquid. Evrain breathed in deeply and gave a satisfied sigh. "Thank you, Lord, for creating the coffee bean. This is truly a religious experience." He took a small sip then paused thoughtfully. "What I'm about to tell you my grandmother told me, so much of this I haven't experienced first-hand yet. I've no reason to doubt anything she told me. Witches and warlocks have been around for thousands of years. The power we wield manifests itself in various ways that range from healing ability, foretelling and weather manipulation through to elemental magic. Healing has always been the most common — the rarest is elemental magic, which is only ever found in men."

"Do all warlocks use elemental magic?" Dominic could hardly believe he was even asking such a question.

"There are very few warlocks alive. Even fewer linked to the elements. I know of four in this country, including me. That's not to say there aren't more, but if they were active, they would be felt by others with the power."

"And Symeon?"

Evrain frowned. "Symeon Malus is also one of the four. He's very skilled. My grandmother went to great lengths to hide my existence from him until I was old enough to be able to defend myself. If he had found me as a child, I doubt I'd be here now. It's difficult to explain, but she tamped my ability until I came of age. There was a wall between me and the power. Cracks started to show when I reached my late teens but it wasn't until my twenty-first birthday that the wall came down."

"That must have been terrifying." Dominic couldn't imagine what it must have been like to be told such news. To discover such a terrible secret.

"It should have been, I suppose. It was a shock, but deep down I always knew there was something different about me. I never really fitted in with my family. It manifested in something of a rebellious streak." He grinned and for a moment Dominic saw traces of the mischievous youth he must have been. "So when I found out, a few pieces of a lifelong puzzle slotted into place. My godfather, Gregory, is also a warlock. You've met him."

"Only that once. We chatted for a while. He seemed kind." Dominic groaned. "Oh my God, I'm so stupid. That meeting was deliberate, wasn't it? Another step toward Aggie setting us up together."

"Very likely." Evrain frowned. "I didn't know my grandmother as well as I thought I did. From the moment of my birth, she had plans for me. All the visits here, holidays with Gregory, you... All part of her master plan to keep me safe." He reached across the table and covered Dominic's hand with his own. "This isn't the first time that Symeon has approached me, though he's never come here before. He's telephoned, sent letters. I don't think he would have the balls for meeting me face to face if Grandma was still alive."

"What does he want?"

"An alliance. At least that's how he's trying to sell it. He wants to use me. I'm untrained, malleable. He sees me as an easy target. He's wrong."

"After today, he might just realize that," Dominic said, chewing on a fingernail.

"Don't look so worried. The cottage is well warded and he would never try anything in public. Even Symeon isn't so stupid as to expose our abilities to the world."

"The wards didn't help Aggie. What if he gets you alone?"

"He'll try to kill me." Evrain's voice was icy calm. "Today's little visit was just him confirming that I haven't been tempted to stray from my grandmother's path." He stroked Dominic's fingers and gripped his wrist lightly.

"Aren't you afraid?"

Evrain's black hair shimmered as he shook his head in response. "Not for myself." His grip tightened. Dominic didn't try to pull away. "But he could try to get to me through you. Symeon's clever, I'll give him that. Perceptive. He must have been watching you for a while. Not in person of course, that would be beneath him."

"You mean he might try to kill me? What possible threat could I be to someone like him? I haven't noticed anyone following me around."

The pressure on his wrist increased as if Evrain was afraid he might bolt.

"I have a lot of latent power, Dominic. If I was able to channel, it would make me untouchable."

"And you could channel through me?"

"Not without your consent and not without love. I need more coffee if we're going to continue this conversation." Evrain rose, grabbed both their mugs then headed for the coffeepot. Dominic stroked his wrist where Evrain's fingers had squeezed seconds before. He missed his touch already.

"So how does Symeon channel?" he asked as Evrain resumed his seat.

Evrain scowled and took a firm hold of Dominic's wrist again. "He has a submissive little boyfriend called Damon who does anything he asks."

"I can't imagine someone like Symeon loving anyone but himself."

"He doesn't. Damon loves him, that's all he needs. It doesn't have to be a two-way thing."

"Oh." Dominic's voice was so quiet it barely registered. He winced. The fingers around his wrist were squeezing to the point of pain.

Evrain noticed and released him. "Sorry. I didn't mean to hurt you." Evrain wrapped both hands around his mug as if to stop them straying toward Dominic. "That won't happen with us, Dominic. The feelings won't be one-way."

Evrain looked so serious and intense, Dominic had to reassure him. "I can't be certain because I've never been in this situation before, but I think… I love you. I have since the first moment I saw you and you turned me inside out." Every muscle in Dominic's body tensed as he waited for Evrain's response. His heart was pounding so hard he thought it might burst.

"I meant it when I said it earlier, though it wasn't the most graceful admission of my feelings," Evrain replied. "I love you too, and I *am* sure."

"But we haven't… I mean we've not even…" Dominic didn't have the words. A finger against his lips silenced him.

"No, we haven't." Evrain pushed back his chair, then stood, holding out his hand. "And that's something we need to change. Right now."

Chapter Twelve

Dominic took Evrain's hand. His grip was firm and warm but there was no force, no tugging him to get up. He didn't need to be encouraged. Dominic rose in a daze and let Evrain guide him toward the stairs and up to the bedroom. He stood nervously next to the bed, his eyes fixed on Evrain's handsome features. Evrain smiled and the warmth that reached his eyes gave Dominic a measure of reassurance.

"Relax. I'm not going to hurt you. I would never do that." Evrain moved toward him. "I am going to undress you, though, so keep still."

Dominic's knees locked. There was no magic freezing him in place but he couldn't have moved even if he'd wanted to.

"Hey, this is supposed to be fun. Stop overthinking." Evrain stroked Dominic's hair away from his face. "Any time you want me to stop, you just have to say. I can be patient. I want us both to enjoy this."

Dominic took a shuddering breath and forced his fists to unclench.

"I want this. Please, Evrain, don't stop." He reached for the top button of his shirt but Evrain slapped his hands away.

"That's my job. Hands off." First to go was Dominic's shirt. "This dark green suits you," Evrain said, pushing fabric from Dominic's shoulders. "It goes so well with your hair, which I love by the way."

"It's just red," Dominic whispered.

"It's not *just* anything." Evrain stroked his shoulders then planted small kisses along his collarbone. Tiny jolts of electricity stabbed at Dominic's cock at every touch. "It's copper and bronze set alight. Stunning. Just like all this creamy skin. I want to lick you all over." Evrain ducked his head and laved Dominic's nipple with his tongue.

Dominic gasped and quivered beneath his touch. Gentle licks turned to bites. Dominic threw his head back, his balance shot to pieces. Evrain held him safely as he continued to nip each tender bud in turn until they both stood dark and proud.

"You have a beautiful body and I've waited far too long to touch it. Christ, you've no idea how you've tested my patience!"

Dominic gasped and squirmed as his nipples were tweaked and twisted until they ached. His cock throbbed in his pants and he was finding it increasingly hard to keep still. He moaned as Evrain started work on the stud fastening his jeans with one hand and traced the creases at the juncture between thigh and hip with the other. Dominic's jeans fell to the floor and he stepped out of them without thinking. Evrain circled the top of his hipbones with his thumbs. It was driving him wild. His rigid cock bounced, eager to play. Evrain flicked his shaft lightly. Dominic gave a strangled moan, clenching his hands into tight fists at his sides.

"You seem a little…agitated." Evrain's smirk sounded through his words.

"No shit." Dominic's voice came out as a squeak. "You make it impossible to think."

"You don't need to think. In fact, I forbid it. No thinking, just feel. You've been starved of touch for far too long." Evrain patted Dominic's ass, then gave it a sharp slap. Heat bloomed across his cheek.

"What are you doing?" Dominic got the question out from between gritted teeth.

"Just warming you up a bit." Evrain spanked him again. "Making certain that you're not trying to think."

"Oh God." Dominic couldn't understand why having his ass slapped was such a turn-on. "Stop!" He didn't mean it.

"Remember your safeword? I know I do." Evrain said as he spanked him again. "If you really mean stop, then use it." He turned Dominic around and pushed on his back until he bent over the edge of the bed, supporting himself on trembling arms. Dominic clamped his lips shut, determined that the safeword would not slip out accidentally.

"That's what I thought." Evrain's hand was an effective tool. He rained slaps over Dominic's heated flesh.

Dominic whimpered. His balls drew up tight to his body.

"Don't you dare come!" Evrain clamped a hand around the base of Dominic's dick and squeezed.

"Evrain, please!" Dominic's mind wasn't so addled that he couldn't remember Evrain saying he loved him.

Surely a lover wouldn't be so cruel? He managed to stand upright and turn around to face his tormentor. "Isn't it time you took something off? I want to see you too."

Evrain shook his head. "No. You're vulnerable like this, naked while I'm fully clothed. I don't recall telling you to get up. Turn back around and bend over."

It was much harder to get into that position voluntarily, Dominic needed Evrain to force him. He shook his head.

"Disobedience will be punished, sweetheart." Evrain grasped Dominic's hips and twisted him round. Pressure on the base of his spine pushed him forward until he was bent over once more.

"Spread your legs."

"Evrain..."

"Do as I say." The words were punctuated by a hard slap that left a burning line across Dominic's ass. "Christ, there has to be a law against having an ass this gorgeous. It was made to be spanked. Your skin shows my marks perfectly."

Evrain moved his hands lower, stroking the backs of Dominic's thighs. Dominic peered over his shoulder to see what Evrain was up to. He was on his knees.

"Uh, what are you doing?"

"You'll see." Evrain kneaded Dominic's ass. He kissed the sore spots, adding tiny licks, then pulled his cheeks apart.

Dominic panted. At this rate he was going to come untouched and before they got to the main event. Evrain blew a gentle stream of air onto Dominic's pucker.

"Fuck!" Dominic gripped the bed covers in both hands, pulling the fabric into messy folds. "Fuck, fuck, fuck." His vision blurred.

"I'll get to that. All in good time."

"Bastard! You're a fucking bastard, Evrain."

"Aw, don't be like that, sweetie. I'm getting to the good part."

Dominic's legs started to shake as Evrain used the tip of his tongue to probe Dominic's hole.

"So tight. Let me in, love."

Dominic's head swam. He was far too close to the edge. "If you keep doing that, Evrain, I'm going to come." He gasped the words out.

"I'm doing something right then. Now quit complaining and be grateful I'm not the impatient type or I might be tempted to demonstrate just how much of a bastard I can be." Evrain dragged his tongue along Dominic's crease.

"You know I've never—" Dominic's words were cut off with a yelp as Evrain pushed one finger inside him, just to the first knuckle.

"I thought that might shut you up. And yes, I am fully aware of your delectable virginal state." He pulled free and released him. "You can lie on the bed."

"You're so fucking kind!" Dominic scrambled onto the bed, grateful that he no longer had to take responsibility for holding himself up. His limbs were Jell-O. "Oh, thank God!" He sprawled on his back and reached for his aching cock.

"Touch that and I'll tie you down and keep you on the edge until you lose your mind," Evrain growled.

"Sadist!"

"And you love that, don't you? Look at the state of you."

It was true. Dominic's cock was swollen and rigid, glistening with trails of pre-cum, his balls heavy and swollen.

"It's not fair, Evrain. You can't leave me like this." Dominic knew he was whining like a sulky brat but he couldn't help himself. He wanted more and he wanted it now. He would have stamped his foot if he thought it would do him any good.

"I *could* strap you to the bed if it would help?" Evrain was all innocence.

Dominic wasn't fooled. He shuffled up the bed as far as he could go before he made contact with the headboard.

"Maybe next time," Evrain mused. He started to undress.

Dominic was entranced by the show, forgetting for a few moments his desperate need to come.

Evrain took his time, stripping off each article of clothing with agonizing slowness. Watching him gradually reveal himself did nothing to relieve the fiery ache in Dominic's groin. Evrain's skin was very pale, his body sculpted and lean – perfect to Dominic's eyes. His cock, impressively large, was bedded in a neat triangle of trimmed black hair. Dominic's mouth watered.

"Can I taste you, please?" He'd happily go to his knees and beg if it got him what he craved. *Evrain would probably enjoy that*. Dominic knelt in the center of the mattress, parting his legs wide. He clutched his hands behind his back and bowed his head. "Please, Evrain?"

The mattress compressed a little as Evrain joined him on the bed. "You beg so prettily, it would be petty to deny you. Lie back."

Dominic fell backward in his eagerness to obey. Evrain straddled him, moving on his knees until his dick was positioned above Dominic's mouth. "Keep absolutely still, love."

Dominic parted his lips. He had to stretch wide to take Evrain's cock. The head was broad, slick. The shaft slipped along his tongue with ease. He registered the salt-sweet taste and held his breath as Evrain fucked his mouth.

"Breathe, sweetheart, I don't want you passing out on me." Evrain pushed deeper. His cock hit the back of Dominic's throat, then he immediately withdrew.

Dominic gagged a bit, unused to the intrusion. Evrain made it absolutely clear who was in control. He gave Dominic the time he needed to recover, then pressed forward again. "That's it. You can take me."

Dominic moaned around his mouthful of cock. He risked a lick, then another. Evrain hummed his approval.

"Very nice, darling, but you need to stop that. I don't intend to come until I'm buried in your sweet ass." He pulled away then sat across Dominic's thighs, pinning him to the bed. He brought their cocks together in a loose grip.

Dominic tried to buck his hips, desperate for more friction, but he was trapped and could only watch as Evrain rubbed far too slowly.

"You are stunning, and I would like nothing more than to pound that beautiful ass until you scream." Evrain leaned over him.

Dominic chewed his lip apprehensively.

"However, you've somehow managed to steal my heart, so you control the pace, my love. I promise I won't do anything you don't want me to."

Evrain pulled a plump pillow from the top of the bed and pushed it gently under Dominic's lower back, raising his hips.

"It might be more comfortable for you face down, but I want you looking into my eyes when I make you mine. Okay?"

Dominic nodded, not trusting himself to speak. From the nightstand Evrain took a small glass jar. He unscrewed the lid. "I made this myself." He dipped two fingers into the jar and they emerged coated with a thick shiny gel.

Gently he pushed Dominic's legs apart, kneeling between them. He swirled his fingertips around the bud of Dominic's entrance. The lubricant was silky smooth and cool against his sensitive skin. Dominic's cock jerked in pleasure. For a moment he thought that he would not be able to stop himself from coming, but Evrain's stroking fingers stilled. Dominic came back from the brink with a pained moan.

Evrain chuckled and coated his fingers with a fresh dollop of gel from the jar. Slowly, very slowly, he pushed one of them past Dominic's guardian muscle. Dominic's channel gripped the invading digit, his body trying to prevent its progress.

"Relax, sweetheart. This will feel good, I promise." Evrain coaxed him into compliance.

Dominic squeezed his eyes tightly shut but he didn't protest as a second finger carefully joined the first. After a moment's stillness, Evrain scissored them slightly, then a little more, briefly scraping the bundle of nerves inside him.

Dominic yelped, his back arched, and he came hard with Evrain's fingers still inside him. Cum splattered his belly. The spasms of Dominic's orgasm had barely subsided when Evrain sheathed himself in well-lubricated rubber and pressed the head of his iron cock against him. Boneless, Dominic had no resistance left in him. Evrain sank deep into his body with one smooth push. Dominic's eyes opened wide in shock, watering at the sudden burn. Evrain froze and gradually the pain turned to a desperate need for more.

"Oh God, I'm sorry!" Evrain started to pull back.

Dominic stopped him, clawing at his thigh. "Don't you fucking dare! I need more... Please, don't stop!"

Evrain hoisted Dominic's legs onto his shoulders and took him at his word, plunging forward to bury himself to the hilt. Dominic did scream then, but it was a shout of pleasure. The burning inside him dulled to a throb after a few deep breaths and he relaxed a little. It felt unbelievably good to be filled so completely, and when Evrain began to move again Dominic's vision filled with pinpoints of exploding light. He lost himself to the moment, and Evrain, somehow sensing Dominic's need, began to pound into him with little restraint. He stilled only when his own orgasm overtook him.

Dominic gripped Evrain's shaft with his inner muscles. He wanted to keep his lover inside him as long as possible.

"Relax, love, I don't want to hurt you pulling out." Evrain withdrew carefully and lowered Dominic's shaking legs gently to the bed. He lay next to Dominic and kissed him with lazy, sated passion.

"Stay right there. I need to make a trip to the bathroom and deal with the condom."

Dominic dozed, a wave of contentment embracing him. He couldn't remember a time when he'd felt so thoroughly content. So comfortable in his skin. Evrain returned and cleaned him up with a warm wet cloth.

Then he got into bed and pulled the quilt over the two of them.

"Are you okay?" Evrain traced the track of a single tear that rolled down Dominic's cheek.

Dominic nestled into the curve of Evrain's neck and hummed his satisfaction. Words were too difficult.

"I'll take that as a yes." Evrain stroked Dominic's hair, lulling him to sleep.

Dominic drifted off thinking how amazing it was that such a hard, muscular body could still be so delightfully soft and warm. Evrain was his. His warlock. His love.

Chapter Thirteen

Dominic woke with sharp-toothed creatures gnawing at his guts. He felt as if he hadn't eaten for a week and his stomach was making its annoyance known. When he thought about it, he realized that he had missed lunch the previous day because he'd been worried about getting back late, then dinner had never happened. The reason for the latter brought a smile to his lips. He shifted and the smile was replaced by a wince, his body reminding him of what he had been up to. The dull ache in his ass made him smile again.

Next to him, Evrain lay on his back, one arm thrown over his head, the other stretched across Dominic's growling stomach. In sleep he was gorgeous. His dark lashes lay on pale cheeks, his lips slightly parted. Dominic caught a glint of green. "You're awake," he observed.

Evrain wrinkled his nose. "Depends. I don't smell coffee. Is there anything worth being awake for?"

Dominic just grinned and burrowed beneath the covers. Even in the dark he managed a direct journey to Evrain's cock. No need to ask for directions when it was standing upright like a signpost. Breakfast could wait a few more minutes. Dominic covered Evrain's stiff shaft with kisses. He left damp trails with his tongue, then mouthed Evrain's balls, sucking carefully. Evrain made some encouraging noises. He lifted the covers slightly and parted his legs to grant Dominic better access.

Dominic took full advantage and he began to bob his head up and down in earnest. Evrain didn't last long. He came with a shout and a hot gush of salty fluid that filled Dominic's mouth.

Dominic emerged from beneath the covers, licking his lips. "Good morning."

"Good morning to you too," Evrain said. "You are stunning all flushed and tousled. I could get used to waking up with you." His smile was lazy and satisfied. "You took me somewhat by surprise. I didn't even have time to wake up properly, let alone steel myself for anything requiring stamina or self-denial."

"Uh, sorry?" Dominic licked Evrain's belly, then kissed his tummy button before nuzzling against his flat stomach.

"Don't be. My only regret is that I didn't last longer." Evrain stretched slowly.

Dominic propped himself on his elbows and drooled at the sight of Evrain's muscles tensing and relaxing beneath smooth skin. His expression must have betrayed him because Evrain grinned.

"You'll have to give me a few minutes. Then I'll treat you to a nice morning fucking."

"No! That's not… I mean, it would be lovely, but…" Dominic ran out of words as arousal and panic fought for space in his brain.

"Are you feeling a little tender, my love?" There was absolutely no sympathy in Evrain's voice, he just sounded really pleased with himself, so as Dominic swung himself out of bed he grabbed a pillow and whacked Evrain with it. Muffled laughter came from beneath the pillow.

"I already came. And you should not be so happy that you gave me ass ache."

Evrain tossed the pillow away. "Sucking me off made you come?"

Dominic nodded, embarrassed.

"That's quite a compliment." Evrain pulled him down into a hug, then rolled them over so Dominic was pinned beneath him.

Dominic shivered.

"You love being held down, don't you?"

Dominic's face got so hot he thought he probably resembled a tomato.

"Hey." Evrain stroked his cheek. "That's nothing to be ashamed of. I love holding you down, so we're the perfect pair, aren't we?" He didn't wait for an answer, just ravished Dominic's mouth with a kiss. Dominic craved oxygen by the time they parted. His stomach growled again.

"Either there's a dog in the room, or you need feeding," Evrain said, rolling off him.

"I'm starving," Dominic admitted. "But let me get breakfast. I brought a few supplies back from my place yesterday so we don't have to suffer watery oatmeal again."

"Porridge. It's called porridge," Evrain said.

Dominic rolled his eyes. "As long as I don't have to eat it again, I don't care what you want to call it." He climbed out of bed. The clothes he'd worn the previous day were clean enough to wear, if a bit crumpled. He'd not been in them long enough to get them dirty. Aware of Evrain watching him, he dressed quickly.

"You're still shy, even after last night," Evrain stated. "There's no need to be."

Dominic shrugged. "It's a bit chilly to stand around naked."

"If I had my way, I'd keep you naked all the time. I'm sure we could crank the heat up in here a bit more, what do you think?"

"I think I'm going to cook breakfast." Dominic ran.

Along with the change of clothes he'd brought back from home, he'd also grabbed bread, butter, eggs and milk as well as the coffee they'd had the previous day. When his stomach complained yet again on the way down the stairs he was really glad he'd spent those extra minutes in doing so. The coffee was a lifesaver. Aggie's herbal tea was fine, in small doses, but his caffeine addiction needed feeding first thing in the morning, and after Evrain's reaction the previous day, Dominic guessed he was also an addict.

Dominic soon had an aromatic brew going, slices of bread in the toaster and beaten eggs in a pan. Evrain appeared after a few minutes. He must have taken a quick shower because his hair was damp. He sat at the table, his expression expectant. "The smells of cooking tempted me down."

"The coffee's nearly ready," Dominic said.

"Don't torture me with promises, hand it over."

Dominic scowled but couldn't hold onto the expression. He smiled. He poured two mugs and handed one over. "So impatient."

Ten minutes later, he placed a plate piled with scrambled eggs and hot buttered toast in front of Evrain. Dominic put his own plate down, then sat carefully. He wished he had a cushion. Evrain just raised an eyebrow in amusement, but said nothing.

"Do you want me to help you move some more things today? I only have one job booked and that's not until late afternoon," Dominic asked between mouthfuls of eggs.

"We never did get around to it yesterday, did we? Still, we were occupied with very important business, on a subject we'll need to get back to as soon as possible." Evrain leered in Dominic's direction.

"You're incorrigible. Try to keep your mind on moving." Dominic crunched on a crispy piece of toast.

"I prefer insatiable and it's your fault."

Dominic gave him a curious glance.

"I think I showed remarkable patience waiting to get my hands on your cute body, but now I need to make up for lost time. There are so many things I want to do to you. Things that will make you squirm and scream from sheer pleasure."

Dominic choked on some toast crumbs. He took a gulp of coffee to clear his throat. "Don't say things like that!"

Evrain pushed his plate away. "We'll get back to the topic of you screaming later, but for now, yes—if you could help me out that would be great. We can get more into your truck than my car, though we'll still have to carry everything down the lane. I've been thinking about it—I'm going to use the furniture here and leave mine. The stuff at the apartment is too modern for this place. It was furnished when I arrived and I've only added a few small pieces so most of it doesn't belong to me anyway. The only large thing I need to move is my drawing board—oh, and the chair that goes with it. Otherwise, the stuff here suits the place."

"They should fit in my truck no problem," Dominic said.

"What about you?" Evrain asked. "Do you have much to move?"

Dominic stared at him. "What do you mean? I haven't agreed to move in here."

"But you will." Evrain pinned him with a dark green glare.

"No! I'm happy where I am." Dominic was tempted to pout.

"Don't test me, Dominic. I want you here with me—it's safer."

Dominic suddenly found the tabletop fascinating.

Evrain sighed. "I can't protect you if you live somewhere else. I'm not happy about you working alone either, but that I'll deal with because I know you love your job. But you will obey me in this, Dominic."

"Obey you? Fuck off, Evrain, you can't order me around."

"Oh, can't I?" Evrain's eyes blazed and his fingers twitched. Before Dominic could move, his chair remembered its origins and branches of oak twisted around his body, holding him securely in place.

"Very funny." He didn't bother struggling, just glared as Evrain calmly continued eating. "Let me go, Evrain."

"No." Evrain sipped his coffee. "Not until you agree to move in here."

"You really think this is going to convince me? Let me go!"

"I'm sure it's the last thing that would change your mind. However, it does mean you have to sit there and listen to me." Evrain pushed his chair back and stretched his legs out. "I love you, you stubborn idiot. How do you think I can ever have peace of mind if I'm constantly worrying about you? At least here I have a measure of confidence that you are safe. You can even have your own room if the thought of sharing with me is so repulsive. This isn't about controlling you or taking away your freedom. I promise." He sighed, and the branches wrapped around Dominic's torso slid away with a whisper.

"You're calling me stubborn? Pot, kettle, black." Dominic chewed on his lower lip for a moment. "I love you too." His voice trembled just a little as the whispered words made his feelings real. "I don't want my own room..." He gave a shy, embarrassed smile.

"Oh, I lied about that." Evrain smirked then ducked as a teaspoon flew in his direction.

* * * *

The day was spent making the trip back to Portland, then to Dominic's apartment above the diner in Hood River. There was a limit to the truck's capacity but by midafternoon they had moved everything essential and done a big shop for groceries. The rest would happen gradually over the next week while they finalized arrangements to hand back the apartment in Evrain's case and give up the lease in Dominic's.

Evrain drove his car back from Portland, trailing Dominic all the way, and left it at Hornbeam Cottage while they moved Dominic's last load of clothes and books from his apartment to the cabin.

"You have heard of an e-reader, haven't you?" Evrain grouched as he hauled yet another weighty box along the lane.

"I've never seen the point," Dominic admitted. "Most of my books are hand-me-downs or thrift store bargains. I like the smell of old paper. Does that make me weird?"

"Yes." Evrain was emphatic.

"Does not."

"Does too."

They both dissolved into giggles on the doorstep.

"Oh my God, we've regressed back to nursery school. What grade is that in your world?" Evrain asked.

"Does it matter?" The bottom of his box chose that moment to give up and a big pile of books landed on the path. That set Evrain laughing even harder.

"You go, you have to get to that job appointment. I'll clear up here." Evrain began to stack the books in a haphazard pile.

"Are you sure?" Dominic felt guilty leaving Evrain with his stuff.

"Of course." Evrain contorted his fingers, whispered a word Dominic didn't understand, and the entire stack of books levitated off the ground. "Paper is a natural material, it's of the earth and therefore elemental. I can handle it."

Dominic rolled his eyes. "Cheat."

"And unashamed. Being a warlock has its benefits, remember what I can do with ink." Evrain grinned as he opened the door and guided his floating pile of literature inside with a gesture.

Dominic recalled all too well the results of Evrain's magical artwork. His cock perked up at the memory. "Now I have to go to my appointment with a hard-on," he complained, but Evrain had disappeared inside the cabin. "I shouldn't be more than an hour or two," Dominic shouted through the open door.

He got a muffled grunt in return and decided that was enough of an acknowledgment.

Dominic walked back to his truck and set off for his one gardening job of the day. A potential new client wanted a quote for clearing some waste ground behind their recently acquired property. The visit was to assess the job and provide an idea of cost so it was unlikely to take too long. It wasn't the most exciting job in the world, hard labor really, but sometimes clearance jobs turned into more interesting landscaping projects. Dominic loved the challenge of designing outdoor spaces to suit their owners. If initial grunt work was the price, he was good with that. Most of the bigger landscape companies in the area turned up their noses at small jobs like this one. Dominic enjoyed the variety that a range of different work afforded him.

Dominic had discussed the job with Evrain earlier in the day. Evrain had insisted that Dominic ring him when he arrived, then again when he was leaving the property so that he would know when to expect him back at the cabin. Dominic had bridled a bit at his overprotectiveness but hadn't made too much fuss — he knew Evrain's motivation was genuine concern for his safety and it seemed churlish to complain. After witnessing Symeon Malus' behavior the previous day, Dominic was a little wary himself.

His client's address proved to be quite remote, well outside the town's borders. Dominic pulled up in front of the property, grabbed his mobile and dialed Evrain.

"Hi, I'm here. It looks like someone's got the restoration bug, the place is a ruin. From where I'm sitting it's virtually derelict."

"Perhaps the new owner wants to level the place and build on the land," Evrain said.

"It's possible. It has a real haunted house quality about it. I'll take a picture to show you when I get back."

"Is your prospective client there?" Evrain asked.

"Well, I can't see a vehicle but there's an overgrown drive down the side of the property so he might be back there already. I'll go take a look." Dominic peered through the truck window. There was no sign of life anywhere.

"I don't like it, Dominic. It could be a set-up." Evrain's voice was tightly controlled. Dominic could tell he was worried.

"I won't let fear control my life, Evrain. This appointment was made weeks ago. I'm sure it's fine. I'll call you when I'm done, okay?"

"I'm not happy about this. I think you should lock your door and drive straight back here," Evrain said.

"It's broad daylight," Dominic attempted to reassure him. "I'm not going to lose work because you're jumping at shadows. And before you say I don't need the money, that's not the point. My reputation is important to me. If I let someone down, news will spread."

"Fine. I can't fight stubborn, but don't be long. I've got plans for you tonight."

Dominic's cock jerked. "Do I get any say in this?"

"No." Evrain chuckled. "You need a few lessons in obedience and I'm really looking forward to teaching you." He rang off abruptly.

Dominic growled at the phone but his cock was still swelling in response to Evrain's commanding tone. "What that man does to me," he muttered. He scrambled out of the truck, shoved his phone into his back pocket, then strolled toward the house. He waded through knee-high grass, following the track of the drive. Two channels were crushed flat, suggesting that a vehicle had used it recently. Sure enough, as Dominic rounded the corner to the back of the building, he came across a black four-by-four with heavily tinted windows. He couldn't tell if anyone was inside. No door opened. No window rolled down, so he guessed not. His stomach flipped a little—this was the part of his work that he hated the most. He found meeting new people difficult, but tackling his shyness was a challenge he was determined to face up to.

There didn't seem to be anyone around as he surveyed the garden wilderness with a critical eye. He estimated that there had been no cultivation whatsoever for at least two years. Brambles and nettles competed with bindweed, thickets of hazel and willow. He could just make out the lines of paths. Different heights in the growth hinted at what might have once been formal flower beds. He snapped a couple of pictures of the house with his cell, to show Evrain.

"This is one hell of a lot of work." He itched to get started. To bring order out of verdant chaos. He didn't want to go poking around in the house uninvited. He'd just wait in his truck for a while in case someone made an appearance. If they didn't show in fifteen minutes, he'd leave a note on the four-by-four and head for home. He stood there for another five minutes or so, then turned to head back to the car.

Facing him was a well-dressed man in his late forties, maybe early fifties. His clothing was completely unsuitable for wading around the plot but there didn't seem to be a speck of mud on him. Crow's feet around his eyes and a scattering of silver in his short, dark hair marked his age. His body, encased in a clearly expensive, tailored suit seemed fit and trim.

"Oh my God, I didn't hear you!" Dominic gasped.

"I apologize for creeping up on you. Sylvester Marks. Very pleased to meet you."

Dominic took the proffered hand and received a firm shake. There was none of the pressured squeezing he sometimes got — this man felt no need to assert his strength. Dominic noticed that he had young hands, completely soft and smooth.

"Likewise. Dominic Castine." Dominic gestured to the plot. "Quite a project you have here."

Marks chuckled. "It is indeed. I should explain. I recently sold my business and I've invested in this place as a retirement project. I need something to occupy me now I have time on my hands."

"It could be a really great place once it's renovated." Dominic could see the potential.

"It is a glorious spot and it will be a fantastic home for when I relocate from Seattle. I have a construction crew lined up but I want the surrounding land cleared for them before they start work. That's where you come in."

"I confess, sir, I'm a little surprised. Your crew could bulldoze the land in a couple of days." Dominic crossed his fingers and hoped that his potential client had more vision than that but he preferred to be honest.

"They could, that's true. I considered it, but I have photographs of how the gardens here were set out before they fell into this neglected state and I want to restore them. I'm hoping that there are traces of the original design under the jungle."

"Oh, there are, sir. I can clearly see hints. There may still be paths and edging stones under there." Dominic didn't hide his enthusiasm.

"So you're interested in the job?"

"Absolutely. I can tot up some figures tonight and have a quote in the mail for you tomorrow. At a rough guess, I'd estimate four weeks' work."

"That sounds great. I'd be looking for you to start as soon as possible. Do you have many other...commitments?"

Dominic wondered for a moment about the emphasis Marks had put on that word, as if it had a double meaning. "I have a fair number of regular local clients but I can fit those jobs around this one. I would keep a detailed log of the hours I spend here."

Marks' eyes glittered. "I'm sure you would, you have an excellent reputation. If I'm pleased with the clearance job, there will likely be a future opportunity to restore the garden."

They shook hands again. Dominic fancied that Marks' hand lingered a fraction too long. He shook off his vague sense of disquiet and accompanied Marks back to his vehicle. After a final goodbye, Marks drove away. Dominic had a last glance around. Dusk had arrived and it was getting difficult to see, so he went back to his own vehicle. He started up the engine to get some heat going, then rang Evrain.

"I was about to send out a search party," Evrain said as soon as he answered the call.

"Not necessary. I'm all done. It could be a really great job too."

"What was the client like?"

"Rich." Dominic chuckled. "He seemed okay, though. Told me that it was his retirement project. He's going to move here from Seattle when the place is all finished."

"Anything odd about him?" Evrain sounded dubious.

"He moved quietly, snuck up behind me and I didn't even notice." Dominic thought about the man he'd just met. He was unremarkable in many ways. "The only other thing I noticed were his hands. Young hands on an older man. He's probably spent his working life in an office. Other than that, he was nice enough."

"Hmm. I want you home where I can see you're okay."

Dominic almost made a comment about Evrain's mile-wide overprotective streak, but resisted. "I'm leaving now. Give me half an hour." He rang off then tossed his phone onto the passenger seat. He clicked his seat belt into place and put the truck in drive. There were no monsters in the back seat, no strange objects in the road, no evil flying monkeys swooping down from the sky. He shook his head. Evrain had turned him into a nervous wreck. He switched on the radio to a country music station and bopped in his seat as he drove. A happy glow of anticipation filled him at the thought of seeing Evrain again.

Bright lights appeared in his rear-view mirror. Dominic checked his speed to make sure he was within the limit. The local cops didn't tolerate speeding on the back roads. The lights got closer. He couldn't make out the size of the vehicle but the driver had his high beams on.

"Idiot. Dip your lights." Dominic tilted his mirror to reduce the glare. He slowed down—there was plenty of room for another vehicle to pass him. He breathed a sigh of relief as the other vehicle pulled out. He kept his eyes on the road, silently urging the other driver to get on with it and pass. Without warning he was rammed from the side. His relief turned to shock. He struggled to control the truck, which careered across the road. He was hit again, this time from behind. Panicked, Dominic misjudged a bend and the truck plummeted down an embankment. Frantically, he attempted to steer but the wheel locked up. All he could do was cover his face with his arms and pray. When the impact came, it jarred his entire body. The airbag deployed, smacking him in the face. The seat belt dug deep into his body.

Gradually the noise of splintering wood and screeching metal faded to quiet, leaving the hiss of what had to be a broken radiator.

"What the hell?" Dominic groaned. He couldn't decide what hurt most, his face or his midsection. He groped for his phone, but the passenger seat was empty. "Where is it?" *Must be in the foot well.* He struggled to release his seat belt. The clasp was jammed but gave way after a few sharp tugs. He shoved at the door. It creaked and moved a couple of inches. Dominic growled his frustration. He swiveled sideways so that he could kick it and he finally managed to get it open, pain shooting through his body. He half climbed, half fell from the truck. He scrambled to his feet, trying to keep his balance on the steep terrain. He ached everywhere but didn't seem to have any major injuries.

The coppery taste of blood filled his mouth but he didn't know whether it came from a split lip or if he'd bitten his tongue. It was pitch black.

The sounds of someone scrambling down the bank had Dominic struggling to take a few steps. A bright beam of light struck his eyes and he was forced to squeeze them shut.

"Sorry!"

The light dropped and Dominic was able to focus on the owner of the voice. Upslope from him stood a dark-haired, pale-skinned young man. He had to be quite short, several inches shorter than Dominic, because even with the slope advantage Dominic could meet his pale eyes.

"Hi, I'm Damon..." The introduction was accompanied by a cocky grin.

Dominic's eyes widened as he recognized the name. He was still staring into Damon's strange eyes, trying to decide what to say when a sharp pain to the back of his head made him fall to his knees. Then the darkness took him.

Chapter Fourteen

Evrain began to worry approximately one minute after he thought Dominic should have returned. A sick feeling developed in the pit of his stomach and refused to go away. As time went on, he became increasingly agitated. He knew with absolute certainty that something had happened to Dominic once half an hour had passed. He reasoned that thirty minutes could easily be used up by a fuel stop, a puncture, or a chance meeting with a friend who needed a lift. Any longer and Dominic wouldn't stay away without a phone call. He knew damn well that Evrain was dancing on hot coals over his safety.

"If he's just late, I'm going to tan his hide until it glows." The cabin felt like a prison. Evrain needed space. He slammed out into the garden to pace up and down in the darkness. The change of scenery failed to do anything to calm him. Every part of the neatly laid out plot reminded him of Dominic. Even as he prayed that there was a perfectly innocent reason for Dominic's tardiness, deep down he knew that something was very wrong. His emotions were out of control so he vented, carefully reaching for the sky before he let go of his power. The wind howled, but soon dissipated. Evrain's despair increased.

* * * *

Dominic didn't know where he was or how he had gotten there. He faked unconsciousness for a while, trying to assess the condition of his battered body. He remembered losing control of the truck and crashing down the embankment. He recalled Damon being there, then nothing. Someone, not Damon, had struck him on the back of the head and they had moved silently into position in order to do it. As silently as Sylvester Marks had come up behind him at the derelict house. Could Marks and Symeon Malus be the same person? He didn't understand how that could be possible but only a few days earlier he hadn't known about the existence of warlocks. Evrain had said that Symeon was very skilled. Maybe he was able to change his appearance.

With slow, careful movements, Dominic probed the back of his skull. His hair wasn't stuck together, so he guessed there was no blood. He did, however, find an egg-sized lump, which, when he touched it, sent bolts of pain through his head. "Bad move. Really bad move." He cracked open an eye, blinking to clear his vision. He was inside a building, lying on the floor in the hall. It was cold and drafty but there was a threadbare carpet runner on the floor, which he was becoming intimately acquainted with. He attempted to get up, making it to his knees before pain wracked him.

His ribs ached, and a quick examination beneath his shirt showed lines of extensive bruising from where the seat belt had dug into him during the crash. He glanced around, hoping to find an escape route while he was alone. Perhaps he could make it to the front door if his captors thought he was still safely unconscious.

He forced his abused limbs to move but, as he rose, Damon appeared from a door at the end of the hall. Dominic ran but he was too slow. Damon caught up with him and tackled him to the floor. Damon got in a couple of vicious kicks before Dominic could get back up. He managed to plant a heavy, retaliatory fist into Damon's smug face before a punch to his side sent searing agony through him. He collapsed once more, taking shuddering, painful breaths.

"So stupid. What does Evrain see in you?" Damon produced two lengths of rope and tied Dominic up, hands behind his back and ankles crossed. "Be a good boy while I let Symeon know you're awake." Damon disappeared, leaving Dominic on the hall floor.

Dominic sobbed, partly from frustration, partly from pain. He tugged on his bonds but they were immoveable.

When he returned a few minutes later, Damon was accompanied by Dominic's prospective client, Sylvester Marks.

"I don't understand," Dominic mumbled, rolling onto his side to get a better view.

Marks smiled, the expression so cold Dominic shivered. As Dominic watched, Marks' body shimmered, his face became blurred. Dominic shook his head, wondering if the bang on the head had affected his eyesight, but Marks' face gradually resolved into something new. Marks was Symeon Malus.

I was right. Fuck, what an idiot. I knew there was something off about him.

"A simple glamor," Symeon explained. "When you can manipulate the air itself, it's easy to make people see what you want them to see."

The blond-haired warlock looked down on Dominic with barely controlled glee, an evil glint in his black eyes. Black! Dominic shuddered at how demonic they made Malus seem. Evrain's green-gold eyes were strange enough—Symeon's dark glare was terrifying.

"Lock up our guest, Damon. I need to make a call to our novice warlock, something I'm anticipating will be a great deal of fun." Symeon disappeared toward the back of the house.

Damon pulled a knife from his pants pocket. "There's nowhere for you to run, Dommy, so behave yourself. Then I won't be forced to hurt you," he sneered. He untied Dominic's ankles and hauled him to his feet. "Though carving a few patterns in you would pass the time."

"How did you manage not to stab yourself in the ass with that," Dominic muttered.

"Not a complete doormat, then." Damon shoved him toward the stairs. "What's it like getting fucked by Evrain Brookes? I'm assuming you are the fuck-ee rather than the fuck-er. Warlocks are the ultimate alpha males after all."

"I'm not going to talk to you about Evrain. He's none of your business." Dominic stumbled up one flight of stairs, then another.

"Symeon doesn't agree. Ever since Evrain arrived in this country, he's all Symeon ever fucking talks about." Damon's words had a bitter edge.

"You're jealous!" Antagonizing Damon probably wasn't the most sensible option, but Dominic was fed up of being pushed around.

"Am not." Damon leaned around Dominic to open the attic door. The tip of the knife pressed against Dominic's back. "What's to be jealous of when I have Symeon? In you go."

Dominic stepped into the room. "But Symeon is more interested in Evrain than you."

"Is not!" The pitch of Damon's voice rose significantly. He kicked the back of Dominic's knees, taking him to the floor. "Symeon is going to call your lover boy. What do you think he'll do to get you back?" He retied Dominic's ankles, then crouched over him, drawing pictures in the air with his knife. "What are you worth to him?"

Dominic attempted to get into a more comfortable position, but with his hands tied it was impossible.

"He won't respond to Symeon's threats. He's not stupid." *Unlike you.*

"Does he channel through you yet, Dommy? Do you enjoy the pain? Is that what you are, his little pain slut to be used and abused at his whim?" Damon stood, then retreated to the wall. He leaned against it and began cleaning his fingernails with the point of his blade.

"Sounds like you're talking about yourself there, Damon." Dominic almost felt sorry for him.

"Fuck you. I'll be back later, then you and I will have some fun." Damon's lip twisted into an ugly sneer. He slammed the door behind him, and a cloud of dust from the frame exploded into the air. Dominic turned his head away but still ended up sneezing.

* * * *

When the phone rang inside the cabin, Evrain dashed through the door, not bothering to close it behind him. He grabbed the receiver, almost dropping it in his haste to answer.

"Dominic?"

"I'm afraid not."

The voice at the end of the line froze the blood in Evrain's veins. His voice was glacial as he acknowledged the caller. "Symeon."

"I'm touched you recognize my voice. Isn't it a delightful evening?"

Evrain fought back the urge to throw the handset across the room. "Get to the point, Symeon. I have better things to waste my time on than verbal sparring with you."

"Now, now. Mind your manners, boy. I thought you might be interested to hear about my new house guest, but perhaps I'll call back at a more convenient time."

Symeon's voice reverberated with malice, and Evrain had to take a deep breath before he replied. He had to sound calm. Showing his fury would just make Symeon happy.

"Let me talk to him, now." He walked back outside, receiver pressed to his ear. The small vein at his temple pulsed and dark clouds, the color of fresh bruising, began to gather in the sky overhead.

"So you've worked out who I'm talking about. I warned you, Evrain. I told you to take care of him."

"Put him on the fucking phone, Symeon!" It was a damn good job that Evrain had taken the precaution of venting when he'd had the chance. Power sparked from the tips of his fingers. His entire body thrummed with it.

"I'm not sure that's going to be possible. Mr. Castine is somewhat indisposed at the moment." Symeon couldn't have sounded more gleeful if he tried.

"Put him on now, Symeon, or this conversation goes no further," Evrain snapped.

"Oh, very well, as you and I are friends. Anything to oblige. Damon, fetch our guest. And make sure he is suitably restrained. You are ugly enough without the addition of any more bruises." Symeon's voice became more distant as he addressed Damon.

Evrain took a small measure of satisfaction from the fact that Dominic seemed to have caused some damage to at least one of his captors. He waited impatiently for seconds that seemed like hours.

"Evrain, is that you? I'm sorry..." Dominic whispered, his words tentative. It was the best sound Evrain had ever heard.

"Stop apologizing, you idiot. Are you okay? What happened?"

"Yes, I'm in one piece, more or less. I was on my way back. They ran me off the road. I managed to get out of the truck but they knocked me out. I don't know where I am." His voice shook slightly, and Evrain knew that he wasn't telling the truth about being okay.

"It's going to be fine. I love you. That lizard Symeon is going to pay for this." There was a bit of scuffling and a curse.

"That's not very polite, Evrain." Symeon had wrestled the phone back. "Please consider your words more carefully."

In the background there was the sound of a vicious slap and a gasp of pain. Evrain's fist clenched around the phone, and he swallowed the profanity he was about to utter. Lightning split the sky.

"What do you want, Symeon?"

"Ah, the million-dollar question. Perhaps I should just ask what you are prepared to give me in order to save your sweet lover's life?"

"How about my promise to tear you and your boyfriend into tiny pieces?" The urge to do serious damage had Evrain's fingers twitching. He clenched his fist.

"Damon, you can take our guest back to his room. You may have one hour to do whatever you want to him. No permanent marks, though."

Bile rose in Evrain's throat. "No! Call him off, Symeon. Just tell me what you want." Evrain couldn't bear the idea of Dominic left helpless with Symeon's deranged boyfriend. It was possible that Damon had killed Aggie, though Evrain had no proof. Symeon wouldn't dirty his own hands. Thunder began to rumble in the clouds, mirroring Evrain's black mood.

"Haven't you worked it out yet?" Symeon crowed. "I thought you were supposed to be intelligent?"

"Stop playing games, Symeon." Evrain fought to keep his voice calm even as he seethed inside at his own helplessness.

"Fine, you precocious little brat. There's only one thing that will secure your redheaded angel's freedom. You. I want you. But I'm going to make you wait to find out how you can make the heroic sacrifice. I'll call you in the morning. Sweet dreams." The loathing in his voice was chilling.

Forked lightning split the sky and thunder cracked the heavens as Evrain screamed his fury into the night. He would willingly give himself up to save Dominic but Symeon would have no intention of letting him go. Now he had Evrain's greatest weakness in his clutches, he'd want to keep him, at least until Evrain was no longer a threat. Evrain wasn't too proud to admit he needed help and he knew exactly where he could find it. He marched back into the cabin, slamming the door behind him.

Evrain's mind was in turmoil. He couldn't remember Gregory's number. He swapped Aggie's handset for his mobile and thanked the Lord for speed dial. The call connected. Evrain tapped his foot impatiently as he waited for Gregory or Coryn to answer. He didn't give any room to the thought that they might be out or away from home. He started muttering curses at the receiver and nearly didn't hear when someone finally answered.

"What?" Gregory did not sound impressed.

"Gregory, it's Evrain."

"Oh! Hi, Evrain. Sorry I snapped. Coryn and I were…kind of in the middle of something."

Evrain could guess what that meant, but felt no remorse. "Your hanky-panky will have to wait. I'm in serious trouble. Symeon Malus took Dominic."

"What the fuck! I'm putting you on loudspeaker. Tell us everything."

Evrain recounted what he knew, which wasn't much. "What do I do, Gregory? Symeon said he'll call again in the morning but I can't sit around on my backside doing nothing all night." He threw himself into one of the armchairs by the fire. The dying embers spat and hissed angrily.

"Coryn is already packing. We'll get the first available flight, charter a plane if we have to, and we'll be with you in the morning. In the meantime, I suggest you go and see if you can find Dominic's truck. If Symeon ran him off the road, he had another vehicle. He would have wanted to get away as quickly as possible so the truck is likely still there. Do you think you can find it?"

"Dominic was coming back from an appointment with a client at a derelict property somewhere outside of town. I know which road he was taking. He can't have made it back to town or people would have heard the accident. If he didn't go too far off the road, I should be able to find the spot." It was good to have something to do.

"Even if the truck's not visible from the road, there should be obvious damage to the verge, trees, that kind of thing. Use your senses. The earth will tell you what you need to know." Gregory paused. "Are you in control, Evrain?"

"I vented earlier but it's a bit stormy around here. I haven't flooded anything or set anything alight yet. It's so good to hear your voice, Gregory."

"If he's close, Symeon will be able to feel your agitation. Don't give him that pleasure," Gregory said. "Do you have anything to use as a damper?"

"I don't understand." Evrain had no idea what Gregory was talking about.

"Certain metals will damp down your power a bit. If you can find a bracelet—something of Aggie's perhaps—in pure silver or gold, that should do the trick. Put it around your wrist. You'll probably get a headache but it won't do you any harm."

"Okay. I'll go and have a poke around in Grandma's jewelry box. Then I'll go check on Dominic's truck." Tears welled in Evrain's eyes. He blinked them away. "Thanks, Gregory. I don't know what I'd do without you. I'm not ready for this."

"Nonsense, boy. What are godparents for if not to pull you out of scrapes? Be careful on the road and we'll see you soon. I'll be looking forward to giving Symeon Malus exactly what he deserves."

Evrain had not yet arranged to send his grandmother's jewelry to England for his younger sisters, as stipulated in Aggie's will. The carved wooden chest she used as a jewelry box still stood on the dresser in the master bedroom. He placed it on the bed and opened the lid. The top tray contained brooches and rings, so he lifted it out. Underneath he found a gold watch, various pendants and a string of pearls. There was a charm bracelet, laden with miniature models and a small, square envelope with his name inscribed on it. He lifted it from the box, his curiosity piqued.

"What's this?" Evrain tore open the envelope and tipped the contents out onto the bed. There was a note, in Aggie's hand, and a solid gold bracelet forged from heavy links with a sturdy clasp. He slipped it on, snapping the clasp shut. It fitted perfectly, laying close to his skin. He took a few deep breaths. He felt a bit calmer, or at least a bit less likely to cause mass destruction. The note was very short.

Evrain read it out loud, "Evrain, in some circumstances the power is not easily mastered. This will help. Grandma."

He fiddled with the bracelet, which was strangely warm to the touch. "She knew something bad was coming. She knew!" He tossed the paper down on the bed and went to find his car keys.

Chapter Fifteen

It had been wonderful to hear Evrain's voice, but Dominic didn't want him to do anything that might put him in danger. Symeon had taken the phone away before he'd had a chance to get that across to Evrain. His cheek burned where he'd been hit and now Symeon had abandoned him to Damon, who would probably want to do it again. Dominic's stomach contracted and he went cold all over. Damon looked like he wanted to beat Dominic to a pulp, and Dominic had no doubt that the brat wouldn't hesitate to do it. He would enjoy it too.

Damon only took him as far as the hall where he couldn't hear the rest of the conversation between Symeon and Evrain. After a few minutes, the door to the room he'd just left swung open. On its own. Dominic rolled his eyes. "Does no warlock ever open a door by hand, like the rest of us mere mortals? Who's he trying to impress?"

Damon giggled, sounding remarkably normal, then guided him back to stand opposite Symeon. Symeon's smile was cold enough to freeze molten lava.

"Sorry, Damon. You don't get to play with our new toy just yet. There will be plenty of time for you to abuse him once I have Evrain. Now put him away."

"He'll never give himself up to you, Symeon." Dominic's soft tone contrasted sharply with the cackle that came out of Damon's mouth in response.

"Be quiet, Damon. If you have nothing intelligent to say, and that is more than likely, keep your mouth shut. Your flapping lips are only good for one thing and you'll be doing that later." Symeon's fingers flickered, and Damon dropped to his knees with a groan.

Wow, what a bastard. No wonder Damon has issues. Dominic experienced a surge of sympathy for Symeon's unfortunate boyfriend.

"And as for you..." Symeon's eyes bored into Dominic. "Perhaps it's time I gave you a demonstration of true power." His fingers began to weave intricate patterns and his eyes glowed. Words that Dominic didn't understand streamed from Symeon's cruel mouth and his hair rippled, lifted by a whirl of wind. On the floor, Damon twitched and jerked, his eyes squeezed tightly shut, but Symeon ignored him completely. Dominic took a step back but he was helpless to resist as an invisible force pushed him against the wall. A lance of light sliced through the air and cut into the fabric of his clothes, making a series of long slashes. His shirt then his pants and shorts fell away in tatters, leaving him naked and defenseless. His hands were still tightly bound behind his back, his arms crushed between his body and the wall.

Pressure gripped his neck, pinning him against the peeling paper. Dominic's heart pounded. Sweat broke out on his face. He felt utterly helpless as Symeon took a couple of steps closer.

"I can see why Evrain is so attracted to you, boy. You are very…tempting." He extended a hand toward his cane, which rested on the mantel over the fire. The cane flew toward him, landing with a smack on his palm. He rested the silver end against Dominic's bare chest. The metal was warm but Dominic still flinched as Symeon dragged the cane downward, tracing the central line of Dominic's body until it brushed his cock and stopped, resting lightly against him. He struggled to remain calm but his muscles strained against both visible and invisible bonds.

A strangled objection came from Damon, and Symeon blinked.

"Yes, thank you, Damon. This is supposed to be a demonstration of power. Power controlled by channeling, so remember your place and keep quiet."

Symeon flicked his fingers and a narrow cut appeared on Dominic's thigh. Tiny drops of blood welled up, glistening along its length. Dominic clenched his teeth—he would not give Symeon the pleasure of reacting to this torture. Another cut appeared down his biceps, another across his shoulder and yet another across his ribs.

"You see how easy it would be for me to kill you, slowly, inch by inch," Symeon snarled.

Dominic twisted his body in frustration but whatever held him in place was beyond his strength.

"I have absolute control over your body, boy, I can remove every hair individually, extract every nail, and make you feel like you've been beaten or whipped to within an inch of your life." Symeon made a dramatic gesture with one arm, and Dominic fell. He hit the floor hard, unable to protect himself.

"I think we'll start slowly..."

Within seconds, Dominic writhed in agony, every inch of his skin on fire with pain that started as a mild tingling and progressed to searing heat. He felt like he was being scoured with hot wire wool and there was no escape. When the blackness of unconsciousness came he welcomed it with relief.

* * * *

Dominic came round back in the attic. He was cold, naked and he hurt everywhere. Dominic felt strange, different, but without light he couldn't see what Symeon had done to him. His fingernails were intact — that was something to be thankful for. Determined not to give in to his fear, he put Symeon out of his mind and focused on loosening the ropes around his wrists. He winced and ground his teeth in pain as he struggled to get free of the rough bindings. All he'd managed to do so far was to tighten the knots that dug deeply into his raw skin. He was desperately afraid that Evrain might do something stupid in an attempt to rescue him. The last thing he wanted was for Evrain to suffer just because he'd been stupid enough to get himself captured.

Dumb, selfish pride. I should have listened to Evrain. He tried to calm himself and take in his surroundings. He needed to conserve some energy and engage his brain. There were no curtains at the single barred window, which was too small for him to even consider as an escape route. If he got free, he might be able to get a look out of it and see if he recognized his surroundings. It was high, and there was nothing in the room to stand on, but if he jumped, it might be possible. From his prone position, he could still see that it was dark outside and there was heavy cloud cover, no stars or moonlight. He couldn't have been unconscious for long.

When Damon had brought him to the room the first time, he'd been forcibly shoved up two flights of rickety stairs. The unconventional shape of the ceiling told him it had to be the attic. That made any escape twice as hard. He'd have to get all the way back down those creaky stairs without being heard if he was to stand any chance of getting out.

It took him about half an hour of skin-abrading agony to loosen the ropes around his wrists. He shook them off, then had to wait for a moment as his tortured muscles returned to life with a vengeance, sending spikes of pain through his shoulders. When the throbbing subsided to a dull ache, he tackled the bindings around his ankles. Damon could tie a damn good knot and it took a while to tease it loose but Dominic had nothing better to do. He unwound the rope and threw it to one side, then stood up and stretched. He rubbed the bits of his body that had been in contact with the hard, planked floor and gave thanks that he didn't have an ass full of splinters. He tested the door just in case Damon had been so complacent that he'd left it unlocked, but despite his careful tugging on the handle, it remained firmly closed.

There was so little light that he could only feel his way around the walls. Jumping to see out of the window showed him nothing but treetops. He decided his best option was to sit tight and wait for Damon to return.

He was sure it would happen sooner or later—the little worm hadn't had nearly enough fun with him yet. Damon clearly relished the chance to be the abuser rather than the abused for a change.

Dominic didn't have to wait long before he heard the stairs creak. He sat back against the wall, laid the length of rope over his ankles and put his hands behind his back so that it would look as if he was still restrained. He listened as a key grated in the lock, a surge of excitement rushing through him. This could be his chance to get away. Damon's silhouette appeared in the doorway. Dominic let his head hang forward and remained still. Damon paused, as if listening for noises from the floors below, then moved into the room. He switched on a powerful torch and shone it directly into Dominic's face.

"Symeon made you even prettier, didn't he? He wants you for himself, but I'm going to have you first." Damon nudged Dominic's bare foot.

Dominic gave up any pretense of being asleep. "Did Symeon send you?"

"I'm not his puppet. I have a mind of my own," Damon snapped.

"So this little visit is unsanctioned? You really are an idiot, aren't you? Touch me and you'll have two warlocks lining up to annihilate you. Do you have a death wish or something?"

"Maybe I do," Damon said. He started fumbling with his fly, cursing before putting the torch down to use both hands. Dominic took his chance. He dove forward, grabbed the torch then surged to his feet. He shone the bright light straight into Damon's startled eyes and kneed him in the groin with strength powered by hours of ill treatment.

Damon crumpled instantly into a fetal position, clutching his groin with a squeal. Dominic felt no sympathy — the little shit had been planning to rape him. He raised the torch and gave Damon a firm knock on the back of the head, not hard enough for permanent damage, but enough to ensure that he wouldn't be interfering for a while. Dominic told himself that it was the merciful thing to do. Unconscious, Damon wouldn't be able to feel his bruised balls.

Dominic crept silently down the stairs, moving as quickly as possible. The light Damon had left on was harsh, coming from a single bare bulb suspended above the stairwell. Dominic guessed that it had to be three or four in the morning. Symeon, if he was in the house, should be asleep and even if he woke, surely he'd think Damon responsible for any noise. Dominic guessed that Symeon and Damon didn't share a bed. Damon would never have risked his illicit trip to the attic if that were the case.

Dominic had to try to find some clothes — if he could discover a way out of the house he could hardly run for help naked, although he would certainly do it if there were no other option. On the next floor down, he discovered a bathroom and recognized the ache in his bladder. He made quick use of the facilities, then took a few gulps of water at the sink. He rubbed his wet hand over his face. The cold water certainly made him feel more alert. He caught sight of his reflection in the cracked mirror over the sink. Even in the dim light from the landing he could see that his hair was much longer, unfamiliar dark red waves tumbling past his shoulders. His eyelashes seemed thicker, his eyes a shade brighter. Despite the time that had passed he was still completely clean-shaven — there was no sign of stubble at all. In fact his face felt smooth and soft when he touched his skin. He examined himself with increasing horror as he realized that Symeon had done exactly what he'd said he would. South of his eyes there wasn't a single hair left on Dominic's body.

Nausea roiled in the pit of his stomach. Symeon's casual abuse of his body was a violation of the worst kind. His heart pounded. If Symeon could do this to him with such ease, what else was he capable of? Dominic had to get out, and fast. He shouldn't have stopped. He forgot about searching for clothes and headed down the next flight of stairs as quickly as he could. Every tiny creak sounded like thunder but he reached the hall without incident and the threadbare runner muffled his steps.

There was less light here. Damon had turned on only the single bulb and that was high above. In the dim light, Dominic felt the front door with anxious fingertips. There were two bolts, one at the top and another at the base of the door. Working them back took an age. When he twisted the handle, the door still wouldn't open. His heart fell. He'd have to try to find his way to the rear of the property and seek another exit.

"Did you really think I would rely on manmade devices to keep this place secure? The metal is fused, as it is on every other external door. Only I can release it. There's no way out," Symeon's smug voice sounded behind him as the hall flooded with light.

Dominic pressed himself back against the wall in despair — he'd been so close.

"I do hope you haven't permanently damaged Damon. He does have his uses." Symeon didn't seem overly concerned.

Right on cue, Damon staggered down the stairs behind Symeon. He lunged toward Dominic, only to freeze in place.

"I will keep my overenthusiastic little friend away from you if you come with me quietly. If not, I'll ensure that you are unable to move as he does whatever he wants to you." Symeon tapped his ever-present cane on the floor.

Dominic knew when he was beaten. He allowed Symeon to handcuff him and didn't resist as he was firmly gagged and prodded with the cane while he climbed the stairs back to the attic. Symeon closed the door with a gloating smile, and Dominic sank to the floor. The key turned in the lock, leaving him in darkness once again. A single tear rolled down his face as he fought to control his emotions and beat back his sense of utter despair.

* * * *

Dawn found Evrain pacing up and down in front of the fire. After searching for Dominic's truck, he'd returned home even more unsettled. Dominic had told him he was okay, but it looked as if the truck had hit quite hard when it had crashed. Now Evrain was concerned that Dominic might have serious injuries. He had found Dominic's phone and accessed the pictures he'd taken. The house was just as Dominic had described but Evrain could tell that it was disguised by a glamor spell. There was a slight glow outlining the edges of the building that would have been invisible to anyone but him or another warlock. He yearned to take Symeon apart piece by bloody piece. The man was a menace. He used his powers solely for his own benefit, something that went against everything Evrain's grandmother and Gregory had drilled into him since he'd come of age.

"You should never use your abilities to harm another, no matter the provocation," Gregory had lectured him one day. "There is always a cost for such action."

"What kind of cost?" Evrain had asked, imagining withering away like the old man in Coven, one of his favorite films.

"Your own peace of mind. Use your power for harm and it will eat away at you for the rest of your life. You can defend yourself if the occasion arises, protect what's yours, but use your imagination. There are ways to achieve your goals without directly attacking another."

At the time, Evrain had been dubious. Now, with the man he loved in mortal danger, he could picture spearing Symeon Malus' corrupt body with a lightning bolt without the slightest hint of guilt. Dominic was his, body and soul, he could feel the strength of their connection even in his absence. Their one night together had melded their destinies with a seal stronger than forged iron and Evrain couldn't imagine the pain of losing him.

He froze as a knock sounded on the door, firm and determined, then relaxed as he realized that the wards around the cottage would have warned him about an unwelcome visitor. He flung open the door with a thought and managed a shaky smile for the two men that entered.

"I always knew that being your godfather would get me into trouble," Gregory said.

Evrain accepted his warm embrace gratefully. Gregory didn't change. The silver in his hair glinted in the firelight but his dark eyes still sparkled with vitality.

"Aggie reckoned you were a handful. Too bright for your own good and far too pretty. You do favor her in her youth..." Gregory sounded a little wistful as he turned to his companion.

"He does," Coryn agreed.

Evrain gave Gregory's husband an enthusiastic hug. "Coryn! Thank you so much for coming... I hoped... But this isn't your fight. You got on a plane for me?" Tears welled in Evrain's eyes. The tension of the previous twelve hours broke through the dam of his resolve.

Short iron-gray hair bristled above sharp blue eyes, the lines around them crinkling in sympathy. "You're my godson just as much as Gregory's. And anyway, I was hardly going to let him have all the fun without me!" Coryn gazed at his partner with the gentle affection of a relationship that had spanned four decades.

"I just hope that Dominic and I get the chance to spend as many years together as you two have. I can't bear to think about what Symeon might be doing to him."

"Well, that's why we're here—to make sure that you have a long and happy, uneventful life together! I can't wait to meet the man who has captured your heart. Aggie waxed lyrical about him on more than one occasion and I am most peeved that Gregory already got to meet him when I haven't. He must be very special." Coryn took Gregory's hand.

"Grandma saw Dominic and me as partners long before we even met, Coryn, but her intuition was spot on. I loved him from the first moment I set eyes on him."

"How did he react to discovering your...heritage?" Coryn asked with a slight smile.

"He dug over the entire vegetable patch in a rain storm. I think it's safe to say that he had a bit of difficulty processing the whole concept for a while. Aggie being a witch he had no problem with. He knows you're a warlock too, Gregory, just not that you're significantly more powerful than me."

Gregory raised an eyebrow. "Only because I can channel through Coryn. I can feel the power in you, untapped and unrealized. It's enormous. Far greater than my own. You haven't channeled yet, have you?"

"No. Dominic knows what it is, what it means, but I don't want to hurt him. I have more control just from being near him, that's enough."

"Oh, Evrain, your concern for him does you credit, but sooner or later you will have to channel," Gregory said. "You won't be able to stop yourself, and you shouldn't. We are lucky, you and I, to have found such strong men to love. If he loves you as much, Dominic will understand. If he is as strong as I suspect he is, he will be able to handle the pain." Gregory kissed Coryn's cheek.

"It's not that bad," Coryn said. "I barely feel a thing now, I think I've become immune over the years. Gregory's power is so much a part of me—I'd feel odd if he ever stopped channeling now. Dominic will accept it, just as he accepts you."

Much as he hated to admit it, Evrain knew in his heart that Gregory's words were true. The urge to channel was virtually irresistible. He would worry about that later, though—for now he had to think about how they could free Dominic and put Symeon back in his box once and for all.

He made a pile of toast and a huge pot of coffee. The three of them sat around the kitchen table. Evrain went back over everything he knew. It seemed ridiculously domestic but the normality helped to relax Evrain. Just having Coryn and Gregory with him helped him be more optimistic that things would come out in their favor. For his own sanity he had to believe that it would not be long before Dominic was back in his arms.

The sun was well risen when the phone rang. Evrain answered the call and gave a slight nod to Gregory's mouthed, "Stay calm."

He was no longer alone — seeing Coryn and Gregory together gave him strength and the patience he would need to deal with Symeon.

"Yes?"

"Were you expecting someone else to call, whelp?"

"Charming as always, Symeon." He kept his voice calm and controlled. "Why don't you cut to the chase and tell me where you want to meet?"

"So eager to abase yourself. That pleases me. Do you not want to know how your troublesome boyfriend is this morning?"

"I would rather see him than talk about him."

"Keeping him under control has proved to be something of a challenge. He is rather…spirited. I would have thought that you would prefer someone a little more compliant."

"There is little satisfaction in a tame pet, Symeon. You should know that."

Symeon laughed but the sound was harsh and bitter. "Damon serves his purpose, and he does have a remarkably talented mouth, when he isn't using it for speech."

Evrain winced at the image. "You said you wanted me. I will exchange myself for Dominic but I want your word as a warlock that you will allow him to go free." Evrain gripped the edge of the table so tightly that his knuckles went white.

"My word as a warlock. How quaint." Symeon paused. "Very well, I will bow to your antiquated sense of honor and give my word. Dominic will be freed if you come with me without resistance. Is this agreeable to you?"

"Where and when do we meet?" Evrain asked.

"Do you know the clearing in Belsevere Wood? It's known as Inkcap Glade. It's not far from you."

"I know it." Evrain had been there many times with Aggie — it was her favorite place for gathering unusual fungi. It was a damp, moss-covered clearing in the ancient oak woodland less than a mile from Hornbeam Cottage. "When?"

"Midnight. Don't be late." Symeon rang off before Evrain could say anything further.

For a moment no one spoke. Gregory and Coryn looked at Evrain expectantly.

"Midnight. Inkcap Glade."

Gregory gave a small smile. "Symeon always did err toward the melodramatic. However, this time it works to our advantage. If you can stick to your role as nice, tasty bait, it will be easy for Coryn and I to get into position unseen."

Evrain nodded and ran a hand through his hair with a tired sigh. "I just want this to be over. I want Dominic back so I can lock him up somewhere nice and safe."

Coryn chuckled. He laid a comforting hand on Evrain's shoulder. "You should get some rest. I don't suppose you slept at all last night?"

"I couldn't. Every time I closed my eyes I imagined the most terrible things." Evrain blinked. He had to believe Dominic was okay or he'd lose his mind.

"This should help." Gregory sprinkled a pinch of dark powder into the remains of Evrain's drink. "Go to bed. You're useless to us if you are too exhausted to think straight. We'll wake you in plenty of time."

"Okay." Evrain swallowed the last of his tea with a grimace. "Ugh! That's disgusting!"

Gregory laughed. "You've gotten too used to Aggie's pampering, boy. Once this little problem is resolved, you and I are going to have a long discussion about your future and how best to continue your training. That's my price for helping you out. Agreed?"

Evrain scowled as he headed toward the stairs. "Agreed."

Coryn rolled his eyes. "Bribery, Gregory? Don't you think the boy's under enough pressure as it is?" His eyes twinkled with humor.

"He needs discipline. You can feel the power in him as well as I, my love. Aggie gave him a good start but he needs to be trained by a warlock."

"Well, the lad has my sympathy." Coryn turned back to the sink.

Evrain didn't know what to make of that. He gave Gregory a suspicious glance but his godfather's features betrayed nothing.

"Keep the bracelet on while you sleep, Evrain. You're less likely to drop the place into a hole in the ground that way."

"Got it. No dreaming about earthquakes or sink holes, much as I'd like to dump Symeon into a big chasm and close it slowly." Evrain climbed the stairs, muttering to himself. He didn't know what Gregory had put in his drink, but it was already taking effect. His head was full of wool and the lure of sleep was strong.

Chapter Sixteen

Evrain came too suddenly, aware that somebody was in the room with him.

"It's eleven o'clock, Evrain." Coryn gently shook him into wakefulness. "You need to get up. You have plenty of time but Gregory and I have to leave now. We must make sure we get to the glade before Symeon. Try not to worry, okay? You won't be able to see us, but we will be there." Coryn gave his arm a soft pat then slipped away.

Evrain levered himself out of bed. He didn't feel groggy, just a little disconnected. It was as if the real world had been suspended, frozen in a little bubble of time while this business between himself and Symeon played out. He took a quick shower, dried off then pulled on his clothes. He chose an all-black outfit of T-shirt and leather jacket over jeans. Symeon wasn't the only one who could be melodramatic and Evrain wanted to make an impression.

Down in the kitchen, he ate a snack of bread and cheese because Gregory had told him to eat something, however nervous he felt. It proved to be good advice because the simple food settled his stomach. At eleven-thirty exactly, he set off down the lane. The summer night was clear, the air crisp and chill enough that his breath steamed. The sky was a black velvet blanket pierced with the tiny twinkles of a few scattered stars but there was no moon.

During Evrain's childhood stays at the cabin, Aggie had often taken him to Inkcap Glade. Usually at dawn, with glittering dew heavy on the grass. At night there was a whole different atmosphere. Forbidding was the word that came into Evrain's head as he walked firstly along the river, then into Belsevere Wood. The wood was a tangle of shadows and gloomy darkness, hidden away from the world about it by saplings and shrubs that were contorted and intermingled to form a dense, virtually impenetrable maze. The ancient oaks grew gnarled and twisted, their limbs reaching out with grasping hands. Underfoot, a thick carpet of leaf litter decayed slowly, giving it a spongy feel that sucked Evrain's feet down and soaked his boots.

Evrain followed a barely visible path through the trees. The short walk had a calming effect, and by the time he reached Inkcap Glade, Evrain felt controlled enough to face Symeon without losing his temper. There was little light but Evrain had perfect night vision, one advantage of being a warlock. Despite the fact that he could see everything with remarkable clarity, there was no sign of Coryn or Gregory and he knew they would not be seen unless they chose to be. He sat on a fallen trunk and waited, fiddling with the gold band around his wrist.

Symeon was fifteen minutes late. No doubt a deliberate ploy to get Evrain worked up. A torch flickered through the trees and Damon appeared first, coming from the opposite end of the clearing. He held a lead that ended in a choke chain around Dominic's neck. Evrain swallowed—Dominic looked so desperate. His hands were cuffed behind him and he moved as if he were in pain. He was wearing a pair of old overalls and no shoes, his bare feet dirty and grazed. He glanced up and met Evrain's eyes. At that moment, Evrain knew that Dominic's body might be battered and bruised but his spirit was firmly intact. Even in the darkness, he could see the spark of flame behind the sapphire blue. God, he loved those eyes. He would do anything to keep Dominic safe. Evrain blamed himself entirely that Dominic was in this position. It was his fault that Dominic had been hurt. More than anything he wanted time to get to know him properly. He craved the kind of connection that Gregory and Coryn had, a love that ran deeper than passion, the kind of love that permeated every drop of blood, every nerve and fiber of their bodies. If the night played out to plan, he would get that time.

Symeon had dressed for the occasion in an ankle-length black coat and pointed boots. His hair gleamed and his black eyes glittered like chips of frozen jet. He took up a position opposite Evrain and pointed with his cane.

"Evrain. I hope you are going to behave yourself? I wouldn't want this night to get…unpleasant."

His tone was so patronizing that Evrain's resolve to stay calm wavered. Storm clouds began to gather above the glade and the wind whipped through the leaves of the surrounding trees. Symeon cast a nervous glance up and banged his cane on the ground.

"Control yourself, boy. On your knees. Show subservience to your betters," Symeon said to Evrain.

Evrain took a deep breath. He stood and took a couple of paces toward Symeon. He pushed up his sleeve a little so that the gold around his wrist was clearly visible, then did as he'd been told and knelt. Moisture immediately soaked through the knees of his jeans. An ominous rumble of thunder echoed across the sky. Dominic wanted Symeon to know that, even with his powers damped by gold, he was a force to be reckoned with.

"No!" Dominic's shout was cut off as Damon yanked on the chain around his neck, but he fought him. "Don't do it, Evrain! I consent, do you understand? I consent!"

This time Damon punched him, knocking him to the ground and into silence.

Evrain smiled. Just a small smile but enough to make Symeon take a pace back. He yanked off the bracelet and threw it to one side. Elemental energy rushed through his body. He raised one hand and twisted his fingers. "I love you, Dominic."

Lightning rent the air and flashed into the glade as Evrain embraced his power and channeled through Dominic's prone form. It felt so good. He could sense every current in the air, every twig, every leaf, every animal waited on his command. He could summon fire or flood, cause the earth to quake, whirl the winds into a tornado, but he didn't. With an immense effort of will he stilled the elements and his own mind.

"I will not attack you, Symeon. That's exactly what you want me to do, isn't it? Weaken myself with doubt. Leave myself open to your attack."

Symeon looked absolutely furious. "Do it! Do it, you little upstart!" He stamped forward, looming over Evrain. He wound a hand in Evrain's hair and twisted, forcing his head back. "I'm going to slaughter you slowly. Suck every molecule of power from your body, then make you watch as I fuck your lover until he bleeds. You'll feel every cut as I flay the flesh from your bones inch by inch."

"Charming." Evrain smiled serenely. "What a fine example of warlock kind you are, Symeon."

His scorn did nothing to improve Symeon's temper. He drew back his hand. Evrain braced himself for the blow but before Symeon could strike, an invisible force flung Symeon away from him and pinned him to the ground.

Evrain got to his feet. Ignoring Symeon, he cast around anxiously, seeking Dominic. Damon had dragged him back toward the trees but just stood there staring as if he couldn't quite believe what was happening.

Symeon forced his way to his feet, his face contorted with anger. "You dare to attack me, to go against everything you've been taught? There's hope for you yet!"

"It wasn't him, Malus, you pathetic excuse for a human being." Gregory stepped into the clearing.

Evrain spotted Coryn hanging back by the trees.

"What is the matter with you? Are you so insecure that one untrained youngling threatens your manhood?" Gregory grinned.

"I believe you've met my godfather, Symeon," Evrain taunted. "He's not very impressed with you."

"You are a disgrace to the craft and it's time you learned to behave yourself," Gregory said.

Evrain looked on in fascinated horror as Gregory and Symeon faced each other across the glade. They were less than twenty paces apart. Symeon's lips were twisted into a snarl. Gregory stood still, utterly calm and implacable, waiting for Symeon to make the first move.

"I am just as powerful as you, Gregory. I fear nothing that you might attempt." Symeon shook his head mockingly. "You are deluded if you think I'll run from you."

"Oh, I don't want you to run, Symeon," Gregory said. "But I will give you one last chance to leave before I make you wish that you had."

Symeon laughed. "You don't frighten me, old man. I'll leave when I have what I came to get."

"Evrain and Dominic are under my protection," Gregory snapped. "Neither you nor I has the right to divert their destinies."

"You always were a soft-hearted fool. Give me the boy and you'll see no more of me."

"You'll be lucky to leave here with your life, Symeon." Flickers of light surrounded Gregory's hands.

Evrain ran to where Dominic lay. Damon knelt nearby — tremors wracked his body as Symeon channeled. Evrain crouched next to Dominic and shook his shoulder. Dominic moaned and opened his eyes. "What's going on?"

"Stay down," Evrain whispered, his eyes returning to the confrontation taking place in the glade. "Gregory is facing down Symeon."

Gregory had moved forward and now stood directly in front of Symeon.

"Go back to the hole you crawled out of, Symeon." Gregory whipped up his hand and struck Symeon a stinging blow across the face.

In the stillness of the glade the sound of the blow echoed. Symeon staggered back in surprise.

Then Gregory laughed. "You are pathetic. Go home."

"Oh, this is not going to be pretty," Evrain muttered. Symeon's features were frozen in fury.

Dominic struggled into a sitting position. "I really hope you have a plan, Evrain. Symeon looks like he wants to fry the entire planet."

Symeon came at Gregory with ball lightning. Gregory lurched back, but raised a shield in the shape of a sheet of water. The lightning burst against it, sending sparks of electricity to earth. Symeon's face twisted with rage at his failure. He stretched out his hand and a huge root erupted from the earth to wrap around Gregory's lower legs like a boa constrictor. Gregory toppled, but even as he fell, he shot fire at the root. It dissolved to ash and blew away in the mini whirlwind that Gregory sent toward Symeon.

Symeon screamed his frustration into the wind, which picked him up and carried him into the air.

"Symeon's losing it," Dominic said.

"Hmm, but not losing the fight," Evrain replied.

Figures of mud rose from the ground and advanced on Gregory. He created a deluge of water and washed them away, but lost control of his tornado. Symeon fell to earth, stopping his descent with a cushion of air.

"The mud figures," Evrain exclaimed. "There was mud on the garden gate after Grandma was killed. Do you think that's how Symeon did it?"

The air cleared. Gregory and Symeon stood facing each other once more.

Coryn edged toward Evrain and Dominic. "We need a soundtrack," he said, his face ashen. "I'm thinking *The Final Countdown.*"

"Wow, you're showing your age there, Coryn. I think it's time for me to do my thing, don't you?" Evrain said.

"Wait, what 'thing'?" Dominic shouted as Evrain disappeared into the trees.

"I'm going to eviscerate you, Gregory. Evrain is a coward. He should fight his own battles." Symeon spat his vitriol. He raised a circle of fire around Gregory, the flames dancing high, roaring their intent.

Gregory's gentle rain turned the flames to a curtain of steam. He darted away and Symeon followed. Gregory whirled around and attacked again, but not with magic. He grappled Symeon to the ground. They rolled and fought, sparks flying from their hands.

Evrain approached from behind, waiting for Gregory to show him that he was ready to put their plan into action. Evrain prayed that he had the strength to do what was needed. He didn't dare glance toward Dominic as he channeled the immense energies coursing through his blood. His resolve might falter if he saw Dominic in pain.

Gregory broke free of the tussle on the ground and rolled clear. He gestured at the sky, and above his head a swirling orange cloud formed then broke apart, soaking him. Symeon surged to his feet, cackling with laughter at the sight of Gregory standing there, soaking wet, a bemused expression on his face. Evrain stepped forward into view. He focused all his concentration on the ground, feeling his way through the earth, seeking what he needed. Fire burst from the ground and he used the power of the wind to send it circling around Symeon's form. Symeon was engulfed. He conjured a waterfall from the air but it did nothing to douse the flames. Symeon screamed as his clothes began to smoke and the ends of his hair caught alight. He tried to squeeze a cushion of air between himself and the flames but it just exacerbated the fire. Finally he tried earth, coating himself in mud. It offered some protection, but in his frantic attempts to protect himself Symeon forgot about Gregory.

Heat from the flames came at Evrain, searing his face. He lowered his head and kept his focus on his task. He had to give Gregory time to finish the fight. Gregory raised his hands and from each fingertip came a stream of light. All the colors of the rainbow came together to form a pinpoint of pure white. He pointed at Symeon and a spear of light, blindingly bright, struck Symeon square in the chest. Symeon screamed and writhed as light enveloped him, helpless beneath the onslaught.

Evrain extinguished his fire and collapsed to his knees. From the corner of his eye he spotted Damon sprinting across the clearing brandishing a knife. A flick of Evrain's fingers ensured that he fell in an ungainly heap as the earth rippled beneath his feet. Damon staggered up. He ran away, abandoning Symeon to his fate.

"Enough!" Evrain shouted weakly after him. "This is over."

Simultaneously he and Gregory relaxed and the glade returned to something like normality. Evrain rushed to Dominic's side, propping him up with a strong arm around his shoulders and removing his bonds with a flicker of fingers.

"Are you okay?" Evrain wanted to touch and examine every inch of Dominic's skin.

"Of course I'm not fucking okay. That bloody hurt!" Dominic turned into Evrain's arms and hugged him hard. "You did it! You channeled!"

"Sorry," Evrain said sheepishly. "The plan kind of depended on it. Was it bad?"

"Actually, no. It hurt, but not nearly as much as I thought it would." Dominic melted into Evrain's arms.

Evrain stroked his hair. "What the fuck have you done to this?" He tugged on a long red strand.

"It's a long story. Preferably a bedtime one," Dominic said with a mischievous smile. "Can we go home?"

Lust turned Evrain's cock to iron. "Absolutely!"

"If you two have finished slobbering over each other...?"

Evrain peered around to find Gregory looming over him, holding Coryn's hand. Evrain helped Dominic to his feet then turned to his godfather. "Sorry, Gregory. I got a bit distracted. How are you doing? Are you okay, Coryn?"

"I'm fine. That was the best fun I've had in an age," Gregory replied, grinning from ear to ear.

"And I'll recover after a couple of decent-sized snifters." Coryn said as he joined them, still pale but smiling. "That much channeling was an interesting experience."

Gregory hugged him.

"Coryn, you haven't been properly introduced to Dominic yet," Evrain said.

Dominic smiled shyly. Coryn shook his hand and gave him a conspiratorial wink. "You and I have a lot to discuss, young man. I can give you all kinds of insider tips on how to keep a warlock in line."

Evrain and Gregory both groaned.

"There are a few things I don't understand about what happened tonight, let alone anything else," Dominic said.

"Well, let's take this party back to the cabin. A celebration is definitely in order, and Evrain can explain himself over drinks and snacks. You do have snacks, right?" Gregory replied.

"We have plenty of unhealthy nibbles for you to gorge on," Evrain said. "What about Symeon? Are we just going to leave him here?" Evrain gestured to the quivering wreck on the grass a few yards away. Puffs of smoke rose from Symeon's clothing.

"He'll live. But he'll have trouble doing more than lighting a candle for the next few years. Hopefully all this has knocked some sense into Damon too and he's run as far away as possible. Symeon won't be able to channel. He'll have to get used to being a mere mortal. One that can hitch a damn ride. Come on. Time to go home."

Together, they walked through the woods to where Gregory and Coryn's rental vehicle was parked. Gregory drove with Coryn riding shotgun. Evrain and Dominic cuddled close in the back, Dominic's head resting on Evrain's shoulder. Despite their victory over Symeon, the atmosphere during the drive was subdued. For one, Evrain found the 'what if?'s going over and over in his head. So many things could have gone wrong. Any of them could have been killed. It brought home just how heavy the responsibilities he shouldered were—to manage the power he wielded and to take care of Dominic.

The cabin felt like home. Gregory wiggled his fingers and soon a fire roared in the hearth and soup bubbled merrily on the stove. Evrain dug out chips and cookies.

They sat around the table for a while, ate, drank and rebuilt their energy levels.

Dominic was the one to push his bowl away first. "So, who's going to tell me how the three of you pulled off that show tonight? Symeon was so confident that you would give in, Evrain. He kept going on and on about outdated values and how it was against your misguided principles to use the power for violence."

"Which is exactly why Evrain didn't make the first move. I could then step in to defend him," Gregory said.

"And Evrain defended you!" Dominic exclaimed.

"Exactly. I had to let Symeon believe he'd got the better of me," Evrain explained. "Though kneeling for that man destroyed a piece of my soul."

"But that doesn't explain why Symeon had so much trouble with the fire Evrain threw at him," Dominic said.

"I have a very clever godson," Gregory said. "Our mastery of the elements varies. Fire is an obvious weapon and Evrain is very strong in that power. It's the easiest to control. He knew he had to use a different element to beat Symeon."

"And it was you that got me thinking, love." Evrain took Dominic's hand across the table, intertwining their fingers.

"How on earth did I do that?" Dominic asked.

Evrain chuckled. "Earth. That was the key. You're always going on about minerals in the soil, acidity, that kind of thing, and it got me thinking. What if there was a material, deep in the earth, that would react violently if it was brought to the surface. I did a bit of research."

"And discovered that cesium ignites on contact with the air," Gregory continued. "Evrain drew cesium from the earth and pulled it into a funnel of air around Symeon. It ignited, effectively sealing him in a tunnel of fire. His immediate reaction was to defend himself with water, but cesium explodes on contact with water. By the time Symeon realized that he wasn't dealing with ordinary fire and used earth to defend himself he had lost all focus. It all happened in a matter of seconds, but it was enough time for me to hit him with a bolt of pure light, one of the few things that can reduce a warlock's power. The little cloudburst I created over my head that Symeon found so amusing wasn't water, it was mineral oil, something that protects against cesium."

"You are all amazing. You too, Coryn. Gregory was channeling for a long time."

Coryn shrugged. "After so many years of putting up with him, I'm used to it."

"Hey!" Gregory protested.

Dominic dissolved into laughter, then fought back a huge yawn.

"And that's our signal to make a hasty exit," Coryn said. He stood, pulling Gregory up with him. "I have a particularly swanky hotel booked in Portland. We'll be staying for a couple of days."

"Then you must come back for dinner tomorrow evening," Evrain said.

Dominic nodded. "Yes, then Coryn can tell me all those secrets he promised me."

* * * *

Coryn and Gregory had disappeared to their hotel with a vow to return the next day. It was almost three in the morning by the time Dominic and Evrain reached their bedroom. Though he would have preferred to tumble into bed, Dominic insisted on a shower. He had to scrub himself clean, lose the contamination of Symeon's touch from his skin. Evrain sat on the side of the tub while he showered, soaping a sponge and running it over Dominic's body with gentle tenderness.

"I'm not the same, Evrain. Symeon...did things to me. He made me look different."

"You're still you, the man I love. We'll save a fortune on razor blades."

Evrain's words were soothing. "You can't fix me? Put me back how I was?"

"Sorry, love. Another warlock's work can't be undone. Symeon broke every unwritten law of magic when he altered you against your will. After today, our only comfort is that he'll never be able to do it again."

"Are you sure?"

"As much as I can be. He won't regain his full powers for decades and warlocks aren't immortal. We live long lives because we don't get sick, but nothing too far out of the ordinary."

Dominic stepped out of the tub. Evrain wrapped him in a warm towel and patted him carefully.

"You have quite a few cuts and bruises," he stated.

"That's all they are. Nothing that won't heal in a few days. I gave Damon a few marks as well." Dominic grinned.

"Never again, Dominic. If I have to wrap you in cotton wool and lock you in the cabin, nothing will ever hurt you again." Evrain took his hand and led him back to bed. He tucked him in then undressed quickly. They lay side by side under the covers, not touching. Tension practically vibrated from Evrain's body.

"Is channeling for the first time like losing your warlock virginity?" Dominic asked. "Are you too sore to touch me?" He projected as much naïve innocence into his voice as he could manage.

He gasped as Evrain rolled over him, pinning him down. Suddenly Evrain's hands were everywhere, stroking and touching, his kisses urgent and demanding. "You feel so soft and smooth." He tangled his fingers into Dominic's hair.

"Not totally soft," Dominic whispered. His dick was so hard it ached and his ass seemed to be throbbing in time to his racing heartbeat, begging to be filled. "I need you in me, Evrain."

"Patience." Evrain threw the covers back and knelt, dipping his head to suck gently on first one nipple then the other. When they had hardened he got rougher, twisting and pulling with his teeth.

Dominic moaned and bucked. Evrain shifted his attention to lower down Dominic's body, licking the smooth, hairless skin of his belly while pushing his legs farther apart. He channeled and tiny sparks flittered around Dominic's cock and balls.

"Does it hurt too much?" he demanded.

"No!" Dominic gasped at the combined sensation of pain and pleasure. "It feels amazing!"

Evrain pushed a lubed finger into Dominic's channel, quickly followed by a second. There was a thump as what Dominic guessed must be the jar of lube hit the floor.

"Fuck!" Evrain groped down the side of the bed.

"Enough, Evrain. For Christ's sake, fuck me!" Dominic could do without any more lubrication if it meant he got Evrain's cock inside him sooner.

Evrain lifted his hips and pressed the head of his swollen cock against Dominic's entrance.

"Trust me?"

"Yes! Damn it, Evrain..."

Evrain sank deep inside him with a sigh as little sparks tortured Dominic's cock and teased his swollen nipples.

"I can sense every emotion you're feeling, every pulse of pleasure."

He began to move faster, harder, hoisting Dominic's legs onto his shoulders to get deeper access. They came together in a mental and physical explosion of ecstasy that left them both quivering from a series of aftershocks.

Evrain rolled onto his back. "I'm not sure I can survive doing that too often!" He turned back to kiss Dominic gently, nipping at his lower lip.

"Once or twice a day should be fine..." Dominic grinned.

"Hey, I'm the demanding one, remember? You're supposed to be sweet and shy." Evrain narrowed his green-gold eyes.

Dominic fluttered his lashes and chewed on his lower lip.

Evrain gave an exasperated sigh. "Sometimes I wonder which one of us is the warlock. You've cast your spell over me, that's for sure."

Dominic snaked his hand below the covers and grasped Evrain's semi-hard cock. "Well, witchy boy, I'm about to work some more magic!"

Epilogue

"Evrain, please! You don't play fair!" Dominic's voice was a study in indignant exasperation.

"What's the matter, my love? Are you uncomfortable?" Evrain circled the fallen tree trunk, admiring Dominic's naked form from every angle. Christ, he looks delicious tied down that way, legs spread wide across the rough bark, smooth creamy ass nicely exposed. He flicked his fingers and a few more twists of ivy wound themselves around wrists already tightly restrained.

Dominic turned his head to the side, his cheek pressed against the wood beneath him. Evrain winked at him. "How does it feel, love? The knots and whorls of the bark press into your bare skin, don't they? Does it make you hard?"

Dominic scowled but Evrain knew he'd hit home. Bindweed and creepers circled Dominic's waist and gripped his ankles, holding him firmly in position. "You are hot as hell."

"This is so fucking humiliating." Dominic shifted.

"I suppose it could be considered so, but I'll bet you're rock hard, which can't be comfortable."

"If your dick was trapped between your body and unyielding wood, you wouldn't find it amusing," Dominic protested.

"I warned you what I would do if you disobeyed me, Dominic. You need to learn to accept the consequences of your actions." Evrain gave Dominic's exposed ass a firm slap.

"Let me go, you bastard! I stepped outside the gate for all of three minutes!"

"And that was three minutes too long. I told you not to go out there. I'm sure we're being watched and until I know by whom and why, you are confined to the house and grounds unless I'm with you."

"You don't own me, Evrain." Dominic pulled helplessly against his bonds but couldn't break any of the wiry stems, strengthened as they were by magic. Having a warlock for a boyfriend put him at a significant disadvantage at times like these.

Evrain watched him wriggle and licked his lips as Dominic's dark copper hair tumbled around his smoothly muscled shoulders. He would never forgive Symeon for the torture he had put Dominic through, but he couldn't deny that the end result was stunning. Dominic had already been good looking, but by the time Symeon had finished with him he was beautiful. It just made Evrain's need to protect him even stronger.

He moved to stand where Dominic could see him and slowly unbuttoned his black shirt. "Is obedience really so hard for you?" He shrugged the fabric away from his shoulders and used a nearby sapling as a clothes hanger. He sat on the fallen trunk and ran his fingers through Dominic's gloriously soft hair. He petted him for a while, then bent to remove his shoes and socks.

"Is treating me like an adult so fucking impossible for you?"

Evrain dropped his pants, pushed down his underwear then straddled the trunk in front of Dominic's face. His rigid cock settled against a patch of deep green moss, scant millimeters from moist, parted lips.

"I wouldn't be doing this if you weren't all grown up, my love." He loosened Dominic's bindings enough that he could lift his head and shoulders and rest his forearms on the trunk, then edged even closer. "And you're wrong. I do own you." He pushed forward until the thick length of his cock disappeared into a willing mouth. He leaned back with a moan as Dominic's warm tongue rasped across his sensitive flesh. "You belong to me, Dominic, and you know it."

Dominic didn't stop what he was doing to answer. In the heat of that moment, Evrain belonged to Dominic too. His entire body was controlled by the action of Dominic's lips, his tongue. Handing over control just for a little while felt good. Evrain pulled away from him. Dominic's teeth scraped sensitive flesh as he withdrew.

"Fuck, you are far too good at that!" Evrain held still for a few trembling moments, bringing himself under control, then he dismounted the log and moved to straddle it again, this time behind Dominic. He was so hard it hurt but he wanted to savor the moment. He leaned forward and pressed the length of his body onto Dominic's back, enjoying the warm smoothness of his skin. He nibbled tiny kisses down the length of his spine then sank his teeth into the creamy mound of a firm buttock. Dominic squirmed, as much as he was able, tied down as he was, and Evrain tortured him further by licking the muscular curve. He kneaded flesh with probing thumbs, feathering his fingers across the exposed bud of a tight entrance.

"Evrain, I swear… If you make me wait any longer!"

Evrain smiled wickedly. "I thought you wanted me to let you go? You know I wouldn't dream of doing anything you didn't want me to. Perhaps you'd prefer…"

"Evrain!" Dominic was almost sobbing with frustration.

Evrain pressed the moist head of his engorged cock against Dominic's entrance. "Tell me what I want to hear, Dominic." His voice was calm as he twitched his fingers and a smooth sap rose from the bark of the tree. He collected some onto his fingers and spread it around his dick. He dribbled a little down Dominic's crack, then spread it slowly with his fingertips, making sure he coated his target thoroughly.

"Fuck!"

"Tell me! Or I'll leave you like this for the next hour," Evrain declared. The threat was hollow and they both knew it, but it was part of the game.

"All right! I'm yours. I belong to you, God help me!"

"Better, and about time." Evrain shunted forward and plunged his dick into Dominic's receptive channel, gripping his narrow hips tightly to give himself more momentum. There was no more time for words. His entire focus was on the pounding he was delivering to Dominic's ass. "So tight." Evrain grunted at the force he had to employ, ramming into him again and again. His balls drew up, hot and tight.

When Dominic whimpered beneath his onslaught, Evrain came, hard and fast. He just maintained enough presence of mind to loosen the tight bindings so that Dominic could raise his hips and free his trapped cock. He came instantly, with a cry of release and a sigh of absolute relief, then collapsed back onto the wood beneath him.

For a few moments the only sound was that of rapid breathing.

"Do you think you could possibly let me go now?" Dominic found his voice.

Evrain chuckled and the green ties slithered away. Dominic sat up shakily. Evrain wrapped his arms around his lover, pressed a kiss against his neck. "Forgive me?"

Dominic turned to look into Evrain's eyes and shook his head with resignation. "Why? Will it stop you doing it again?"

"Of course not." Evrain stood and stretched, knowing the sight of his lean body would distract Dominic from his irritation. He took his time dressing then ran a hand through hair that brushed his collar. "I have to get ready for Gregory, he'll be here soon and if I'm not prepared, he'll have my hide."

Dominic grinned. "Don't look to me for sympathy after what you just did! Gregory does has some very innovative ways of punishing you—perhaps if I have a word with him…"

Evrain shivered. "Don't you dare! He doesn't need any more excuses to find fault with me."

"Now you know how I feel." Dominic picked up his clothes, which were lying in a tangle of bindweed. "It's somewhat disconcerting to be at the mercy of every piece of surrounding greenery."

"Dominic...you would tell me...if anything I did ever really upset you?" Evrain needed reassurance that he wasn't the only one who'd had a good time.

Dominic turned startled blue eyes toward him, as he shrugged into his T-shirt.

"Yes, of course I would. I never have, though, have I? That should tell you how I feel. It's still hard to admit to enjoying the way you treat me." He ducked his head shyly. "I love you, Evrain."

A sudden gust of wind lashed the branches in nearby trees. Evrain pulled Dominic into a hard embrace and subjected him to a kiss that left him gasping for air.

"I love you too." Evrain's voice vibrated with passion. "I don't deserve you." He sighed. "Symeon will seek revenge and I'm positive he wasn't working alone. Damon has disappeared. My grandmother's killer has yet to be caught and we are being watched, I'm sure of it. It's not the best start to the rest of our lives."

"We have time, love." Dominic soothed him. "We'll deal with whatever faces us together."

"And, in the meantime, I must face Gregory." Evrain groaned. "Will you be okay while I channel?"

"Of course. Aren't I always?" Dominic nuzzled his shoulder. "Then this evening we can relax, snuggle in front of the fire."

"And I can tie you up, spank you," Evrain said.

Dominic wiggled in his arms. Interesting bits of their bodies rubbed together.

"Fuck you until you scream," Evrain added.

"Are you asking me or is this some kind of warlock prediction? I didn't know you had the power to see the future."

"Where your ass is concerned, the future is not that difficult to see." Evrain gave Dominic's behind a good squeeze. "Gregory is bound to tell me I don't practice enough. I can strap you to our bed and use each of the elements in turn to torment you."

Dominic shivered.

"There have to be some advantages to being a warlock, after all."

About the Author

Lucinda lives in a small village in the English countryside, surrounded by rolling hills, cows and sheep. She started writing to fill time between jobs and is now firmly and unashamedly addicted.

She loves the English weather, especially the rain, and adores a thunderstorm. She loves good food, warm company and a crackling fire. She's fascinated by the psychology of relationships, especially between men, and her stories contain some subtle (and some not so subtle) leanings towards BDSM.

L.M. loves to hear from readers. You can find her contact information, website details and author profile page at http://www.pride-publishing.com.